Penguin Books

**We Hate Humans**

David Robins was born in London in 1944. He is the
co-author, with Philip Cohen, of *Knuckle Sandwich: Growing
Up in the Working-class City* (Penguin, 1978).

David Robins

# We Hate Humans

Penguin Books

Penguin Books Ltd, Harmondsworth, Middlesex, England
Viking Penguin Inc., 40 West 23rd Street, New York, New York 10010, U.S.A.
Penguin Books Australia Ltd, Ringwood, Victoria, Australia
Penguin Books Canada Ltd, 2801 John Street, Markham, Ontario, Canada L3R 1B4
Penguin Books (N.Z.) Ltd, 182 190 Wairau Road, Auckland 10, New Zealand

First published 1984

Made and printed in Great Britain by
Richard Clay (The Chaucer Press) Ltd, Bungay, Suffolk
Set in 10/12 Monophoto Times by Northumberland Press Ltd,
Gateshead, Tyne and Wear

For my mother and father

# Contents

# Acknowledgements

My researches into racism and youth politics were funded by the Leverhulme Trust from 1978 to 1981. I owe a special debt to my co-worker, Philip Cohen. Lucy Bland and Rose Ades researched newspapers and other background material relating to football Ends. Daniele Segre interviewed Beppe as part of his excellent photo-documentary of the Ragazzi di Stadio di Torino. Cloe Peploe translated. David Zane Mairowitz translated the Brecht poem 'On Violence'. I am grateful to Centerprise for permission to use poems from *Stepney Words*. Thanks also to Stuart Glasgow (Maryhill), Neil Burrough (Birmingham), Stuart Wooler, Derek Gibbs, Ric Sumner (Moss Side), Ian Franklin, Alan Ereira and Peter Ansorge for advice and encouragement, and to Anna Gruetzner, for her patience.

Throughout, I have changed names of people, streets, pubs, clubs and so on.

## On Violence

The rushing river they call violent
But the riverbed pressing it in
Nobody calls violent.

The storm that bends birch trees
They say is violent
But what about the storm
That breaks the backs of roadworkers?

Bertolt Brecht

# Introduction

'The board of directors, shareholders, they don't know what's going on. They all watch play in seats. They can't see what's going on. Manny Cussins got a big house and he's got money. He don't know. When he were young he might have been at boarding-school. He weren't at a comprehensive. He don't know. They're old as well, and we're all young. They don't understand. Police don't know what's going on as well. When you've back streets the police can't control it as much. They only control it on main roads. They don't know about back streets. They get it all wrong. They think all fighting's done where they are. They don't know about where it really is. Same with newspaper reporters. They can't report it. They're all in wrong places.

'Experts say it started cos of bad housing, unemployment... That's why you get football violence. That's a load of rubbish as well. That's nowt to do with it. When I've been to court, judges say: "Good upbringing, why do you do it?" Everyone says same. "You've got a good job, you've got good school records." They all say this. "Why do you do it then?" And they think it's cos of bad housing. When you go to court they say, "Why do you do it?" And they're supposed to know already! They don't know!'

Sean, aged seventeen, Leeds United fan

This book is based on over seven years of research and several hundred hours of tape-recordings with young people from all parts of the country. It tells the story of working-class youth and the rise of the football Ends from the inside, often directly through the descriptive accounts of the people involved. No panaceas or moral judgements are offered.

Politicians and public figures have not been slow to pronounce on the 'hooligan menace'. Every new wave of riot and soccer warfare revives the Great Debate. Make parents responsible? Bring back National Service? The birch? The rope? Ban professional football itself? More compassionate voices bemoan the plight of the 'disadvantaged' in tones reminiscent of liberal social reformers of over a century ago (only perhaps not quite so well informed). From the right: breakdown of respect for authority and property, and the encouragement inadvertently given to lawbreaking by the permissive culture are responsible; from the left: unemployment and poverty are to blame. All these explanations may contain ingredients of the truth, but this is outweighed by a sickening sense of the values and standards of One Nation pronouncing upon another, as the following example shows.

In the early seventies, when soccer hooligans were being ranged alongside the I R A as Enemies of the People, some young squaddies, about to be posted to Belfast, went to Stamford Bridge to watch Chelsea. Before the kick-off they got drunk in the pub. Inside, they sprawled in the gangway, singing, spitting and throwing lumps of hot dog at the people around them. A policeman made his way through the crowd and threatened to chuck them out. Later, hearing that the boys were due to leave for Ireland next day, the magistrate deferred sentence, commenting, 'You are better employed carrying out your duties in Belfast.'

Scarcely a voice in the Great Debate comes from the Other England (although there has been no shortage of plays and flims portraying, even celebrating, youth violence). Sociologists and anthropologists, such as Peter Marsh[1] and Desmond Morris,[2] have interviewed and observed the fans, only to provide models for theories of 'the policing function of ritual', and to offer yet another example of society's age-old need for a safety valve. 'The Circus Factions, the rival groups of charioteer supporters in the first few centuries AD, behaved very much like contemporary soccer hooligans,' writes Marsh. 'We also have to remember that football itself in the Middle Ages was just an excuse for aggro.' But what's it like growing up amid the pressures and tensions of the working-class city?

In the early seventies I helped organize a youth centre on a large

1. cf. Peter Marsh, *Aggro*, Dent, 1978.
2. Desmond Morris, *The Soccer Tribe*, Jonathan Cape, 1981.

working-class estate in North London.[3] A mile away stood Highbury stadium and as most of our members were Arsenal supporters I started a discussion group around the issue of 'Why football violence?' The meetings were recorded, and I held follow-up sessions with those individuals who were both heavily involved in the action and who also happened to be good talkers. 'When Chelsea come down, we was all packed tight, right the way across ... There was thousands of the bastards ... The tension, it was like a matchstick clicking.'

Sitting around the tape-recorder, the mood was usually relaxed and sophisticated. Most of those taking part were boys who had just left school to go straight into 'crap jobs' or on to the dole. But it didn't matter compared with the excitement of being 'up the End' alongside your mates and up against the others. 'You could have a terrible week, a bust-up with your girl, row with the old man, lose your job, everything could have gone wrong ... But when you go down there, on the terraces, you're shouting along with the rest ... Your worries fall away, you're top of the world.'

The various street gangs that made up part of the Arsenal North Bank were described. 'The Kington ... see 'em walking down the street, four or five abreast, crop-heads, crombies, Doc Martens and the rest. Old folks stepping off the pavement to let 'em pass. All they care about is looking *hard*. And for that minute nothing else matters.'

How many brothers had Charley Tappin of the West Ham North Bank? Did the Sheriff really take on fifty of the Crystal Palace Eagles singlehanded? What really happened when the Butcher of Shepherd's Bush Green strangled a chicken up the Park Lane Tottenham? Listening to these accounts, a picture emerged of a whole under-life, beyond all forms of official control. 'We hate humans,' Manchester Uniteds fans chanted after being called 'animals' in the press.

I went on to visit the major footballing cities, and, with the help of friendly fellow-teachers and youth-workers, built up a net-work of contacts among young fans. Some followers of Manchester United came from as far apart as Dover and Carlisle. In some

3. An experience described in David Robins and Philip Cohen, *Knuckle Sandwich: Growing up in the Working-class City*, Penguin, 1978.

neighbourhoods the soccer End provided a focus through which one could glimpse something of the broader predicaments of local youth (unemployment and the Liverpool Kop, for example). In Oakdale, a huge housing estate outside Portsmouth, I sat on a youth club brains trust, a bizarre evening, where the chairman, a muscular Christian, advised an audience fresh from smashing up a soccer special to take up squash as an alternative. (The 'I'm Backing Britain' campaign started there in the sixties. Today it is a region badly hit by the recession.)

Following my travels I compiled a soccer fans' geography of Britain, an A–Z of the Ends. Each entry includes notes on size, track record, social background and any distinctive features. For example, Crystal Palace used to be the meeting-place for South London bikers; the Park Lane shows a strong black and white mix. In fact, although the character of the End may vary greatly according to locality, in the big cities one underlying factor that determines the pattern of recruitment is always the same: in Birmingham, London and Liverpool old neighbourhoods that have long been centres of support for the big clubs have been broken up, whether through urban redevelopment or through dramatic changes in local patterns of employment. One consequence is that many children of life-long supporters no longer grow up in the old city centres but in suburbs, over-spills, new towns – places that were never designed for anybody who wanted to move out of a living-room, let alone go to a soccer match. Outer London suburbs such as Borehamwood, or the massive Chelmsley Wood estate near Birmingham, were designed for the family, for *internal immigration*, and there are no natural mass meeting-places. But for the young, growing vegetables in the back-garden in Chingford is not a sufficient communal substitute. So they come back to the old parts of the cities where the soccer grounds are located: 'In our city home', 'United' once more, as if by magic. 'They all shout "Portsmouth" together ... otherwise it's still all different communities ... But at a big match we're all a big community then.'

For some young people, being a supporter is in the blood, passed down through the family, like religion or politics. Soccer, playing and watching, has long been a vital part of the schoolboy Saturday, an escape from the boredom and irrelevance of the classroom. But in the late sixties a new element, aggro, was born on the North Bank.

From woolly hats and rattles to belts, boots and braces. The new scene also pulled in girls in rolled-up white jeans and Doc Martens. Some still conformed to a feminine stereotype of involvement – girls would be content with just meeting the player they had worshipped for so long. Others joined in the aggro. As one lad put it: 'There was this fuckin' great big girl, Linda. She must be six feet. She wears a pair of Doctor Martens. This geezer who was pissed tried to grab her. She gave him a right hard punch.'

The origins of terrace aggro are shrouded in myth: '... someone nicked another kid's scarf and it started from there!' Yet violence at football grounds is not new. In Glasgow, at the gemme, Rangers against Celtic has long spelled sectarian warfare between gangs of Billies and Tims. Then came the upsurge of working-class subculture of the fifties and sixties; from teds and rockers to the making of a sixties mod; and from mod to hard mod to skinhead soccer fan. A separate history.

You only have to look across the soccer generations to see the change. 'From times I could remember there were scuffles in crowds,' recalls an elderly supporter. 'But it was punch-ups among *men* in those days. It was different. It was rough all right. But I don't think the viciousness was in the air then as it is now.' A community-worker from Moss Side, Manchester, gives his own explanation: 'Look at the concrete flats outside here! Can you imagine anybody looking at them and getting a warm glow and saying, "That's home!" We used to have that in the old – what they told us were slums. I mean at least you felt you were home when you walked down the street. You were somebody. You got a place, you got an identity ... But of course that community was destroyed ...'

Were the 'bad old days' really so good? Admittedly, what has taken their place is harder to romanticize. On one occasion I visited Chelsea when the visitors had 'taken' the Shed (the home End) before the kick-off. The West Ham Mile End had arrived early at the gates, taken off their scarves, and fooled the police into thinking they were home fans. Inside they sang 'In our Chelsea home'. A walkover: the Shed 'taken' without a boot raised in its defence. Towards the end of the match, however, a tense nil–nil affair, some Chelsea boys, who had been forced to the perimeters of their own terrace, launched a counter-attack led by some eleven-year-old kamikazes. This had little effect at first, but when Chelsea scored with five minutes of the game to go things got very nasty, as hundreds of enraged West Ham supporters surged down the terrace, lashing out in all directions. As the mounted police drove into the throng and the fighting spilled over on to the pitch, and innocent spectators held bleeding heads, I felt scared and sick. 'This is crazy! What are you doing fighting each other? What about your real enemies? Like the people over there! ' I pointed to the posh seats of the directors' box. 'Leave it out!' one kid replied. 'They're all just a load of fuckin' yids!'

It seems that the best way to deal with strangers is to kick them in the head. For several years the National Front, known to the kids as 'the violent party', has deliberately sought to exploit the tension between the colour of your scarf and the colour of your skin. Trapped in a high-rise block in Satellite City, feeling 'like baked beans in a tin can', a white skin can become a statement of identity. There are many instances where a skinhead bovver boy has turned into a portrait of a racist. Yet, despite considerable efforts at infiltration of the Ends, and leafleting and recruitment outside grounds (a campaign I document here), the National Front has failed to win a secure base. The counter-campaign of the Anti-Nazi League's 'Soccer Fans against the Nazis' undoubtedly had some impact. But the real resistance came from the kids themselves. 'They think they've got something. Independence. It might not be very much, but it's something. So any bloke who comes along waving a Union Jack and saying, "You're for us, lads!" is bound to be treated with suspicion,' said a school teacher from Birmingham. And it's a suspicion of politics and political manipulation of any kind. When I asked Sean from Leeds what he thought of the NF he replied, 'I hate them! And I hate the fucking socialists as well!'

For the most part I have avoided interviews with the more disturbed and psychopathic elements in the Ends. This is not for reasons of personal safety but because I was concerned to locate the rise of soccer aggro within the experience of the *mainstream* of working-class youth. However, I have included the return of the hard men, many in their late twenties, whose intervention on the terraces decisively changed the mood at the end of the seventies.

It is an open question why Britain, home of decency, tolerance and reserve, should have produced such a volatile, atavistic youth culture. And a highly exportable one. In Holland, wall posters designed by Ajax (Amsterdam) fans invite Feyenoord (Rotterdam) fans to 'come up the F-side for a party. Bring your own bottles, knives, etc.' German supporters visit London clubs 'to see how it is done'. In Italy, Beppe, a leader of the English-style 'ragazzi di stadio', quotes Kevin Keegan: '... in England the most important thing in football is not the players, not the clubs, but the *fans*'.

In England it is hard to see youth culture as any longer representing some kind of brash, self-confident break with the past, as it appears in Italy. Images of youth have changed: from Beatles and Mods, 'clever, classless and free', to the 'sad, shitty seventies' with its racist skinheads and disenchanted punks. The riots of summer 1981 saw a new image of the kids united, black and white, in one big mob, and up against the law.

But behind the images perhaps there is something more to riots and soccer Ends than meets the eye. And perhaps that something has more to do with the dynamics of class than it has to do with the psychodynamics of adolescence, the breakdown of authority or the mere vagaries of youth. It is my contention that the cruel banalities of English class life continue to take their toll.

Working-class youth has always been the most exploited, vulnerable section of the labour force, forever in and out of work. Today the massive economic recession means that youth labour is increasingly superfluous. Nearly half of all early school-leavers are without a job. The following account was written by David Roberts, a seventeen-year-old boy on a Youth Training Scheme. It perhaps serves better than most accounts of contemporary experiences to illustrate their predicament.

'You would think this story started when I left school. But it really started just before. Everyone was called to see the school's careers officer, and one by one we all filed in. Although everything about the way you should behave during an interview was explained, right down to the last detail, it was not impressed upon us just what the job situation was – just how scarce jobs were. So everyone I know adopted an attitude of not caring less – just living day by day, not thinking about their future at all – and that included me.

'When I left school an appointment had already been made at

my local careers office. I went up there and met the careers officer, a woman named Maria. But really there was nothing she could do for me. I had only one qualification. She sent me to countless jobs in supermarkets, fruit stalls, shoe shops, etc. But all to no avail. After a couple of weeks, not even being able to get a menial job in a supermarket really got me down.

'I felt like a real fool. The monotony of being at home with no money, day after day after day, was really freaking me out. At first it was a laugh – no school, laying around in bed. But, watching the kids' programmes on TV every morning! It was too much.

'Then my mum and dad started getting on my back. They never liked me sleeping half the day. They nagged and nagged and I tried to explain to them. There was no point getting up. What was I getting up for? Then they started harping on about money. Again I tried to explain. Do you think I'm the only person in the country who is unemployed? Every night on the news you hear about more and more redundancies. Now there's three million on the dole. But to my parents it was like it was just on the news. It never seemed to sink in that this was going on around them. To them it was just talk on the telly. It was my laziness that was stopping me getting a job.

'Time went on and it just got worse and worse. I knew what month it was, but I never knew what day. It had come to the point where it did not matter the slightest. Every day was the same.

'Me and my friends started to do crazy things, just to make the days pass a little faster. We would roam the streets all day in search of some fun. And this led to trouble with the police. It was lucky I managed to get on to a Youth Training Scheme. It may not be the greatest thing in the world, but at least it makes your world kind of real again. It brings an order and routine back into your life. Some of my friends have not been so lucky. Being unemployed has really changed them. They are not the same people I went to school with, the ones that aren't picking pockets or out doing some crazy act.

'But although I am on a scheme, it only lasts a year and there are forty-seven years before I get a pension. So there's a good chance I could still end up in the same boat as the rest of my friends.

'Verdict: Shoot Thatcher.'

# Part One

# Images of Youth

'And you may ask yourself – Well ... how did I get here?'

The Talking Heads

'1953. No unemployment to speak of, a national health service and social security system to soften the old class warfare, a new and fairer educational system, an expanding industrial base, a lead in nuclear technology, a place at the head of a great commonwealth. A new Golden Age?' This is how one writer reflected on the state of the country in the wake of the Festival of Britain.

It was with some suddenness that the acquiescent generation who had survived the war and had their fill of divisive politics were confronted with a new image of violent disorder, the juvenile delinquent. In 1955 groups of teddy boys and girls appeared on the streets of working-class suburbs and the new towns. Now that the bomb sites were disappearing, youth was making its mark with loud music and slashed seats.

Here was some alien presence that had appeared to come out of nowhere. Insecure young offenders infected with a mysterious virus of criminality were being hauled before the courts. Where did they come from? The reactionary media were quick to blame the 'softy' approach of the Welfare State. 'What do they want, coddle-cures for hooligans?' asked the leaderwriter of the *Daily Express*. Some social researchers, however, talked of the disruptive effects of wartime. These were the first exchanges in the great public debate.

A very different image of youth surfaced in April 1958 when the Campaign for Nuclear Disarmament first took to the streets. One observer commented: 'All these young people, it's unbelievable. Aldermaston has started something new, and the sixteens to twenty-threes took to it like the children of Hamelin to the music of the Pied Piper.' Led by veteran pacifists, the ranks of CND included bright young sixth-formers looking for escape from the stifling confines of the grammar school prefects' room, LSE and Oxbridge undergraduates, people bearing historic names, and famous young people from the world of the arts such as John Osborne and Vanessa Redgrave.

By the end of the fifties, the iconography of the the Youth Spectacle was polarized more or less along class lines: a separate development of Angry Young Men, coffee bars and CND badges on one side; rock 'n' roll riots, flick knives and speedway on the other. Few angries had heard of Split Waterman, while the name Bertrand Russell wouldn't have rung many bells in the juke-box cafés of South London.

By 1960, however, the teds had virtually disappeared from public view, and while working-class subcultures continued their separate and uneven developments they seemed to be causing far less trouble and got comparatively less attention from the media than sections of privileged youth, for the latter threatened and sometimes staged disruptions. In April 1962 the annual Aldermaston march of CND had attracted a crowd of over eighty thousand people, most of them young and middle-class.

The swelling ranks of youthful protesters also seemed to be developing a sinister counter-culture which appeared to have more to do with affronting the traditional decencies of English life than with banning the Bomb. Large sections of the great mass of middle-class and lower-middle-class youth, it was claimed, were in reaction to the affluent and respectable homes from which they had sprung, and to the diligent, sporting hearties with whom they shared the grammar school prefects' room. The beard, the duffle coat, the long black stockings ... had become for many signs of the emergence of a whole new generation who, it seemed, would not be inhibited by outmoded conventions or habit from taking a bold and independent view of the world.

It wasn't long before the issue of nuclear disarmament was lost in the generality of this proclaimed revolt against cultural standards: these young people were searching for images of irreverence and sexual precocity which would have far greater appeal than the protest language of CND.

At the beginning of the sixties a new generation of working-class heroes had emerged, mainly through the art colleges, but including actors, playwrights, novelists and photographers. At the forefront of the new heroes were the beat groups, led by the four lads from

Liverpool. Flaunting their ethnic credentials, which were as much provincial as working-class, they seized the centre stage of the Youth Spectacle.

For years, *New Musical Express* had been asking, 'What's wrong with British rock?' and had grumbled about the domination of America over the British pop scene. Now the music industry was satisfied. To break away from their initial dependence on the imperialism of American youth and *its* pop aristocracy, the great mass of middle-class youth had turned to an indigenous image in English working-class youth, who for generations had been growing up on the wrong side of the tracks, the wrong side of the law, and who, as I have already pointed out, had their own subcultures.

The British beat scene had of course originated in tough, ethnic Liverpool, a provincial city that was to become something of a holy place, designated by American youth guru Allen Ginsberg in 1966 as 'at the present moment the centre of the consciousness of the human universe'. Although the Mersey Sound was brash, spirited and proud of its origins, it was hardly tough and lawless. It was prettified, cleaned-up, and mod-suited and hairstyled, with a core audience of largely working-class boys and girls. But the new heroes weren't all like that. Out of the art schools had come members of the ugly, sexually precocious groups, like The Kinks, The Who and The Rolling Stones – the suburban rhythm 'n' blues of Mick Jagger.

The audience these new heroes found was a cosmopolitan mixture, from the children of Beatlemania to older working youth and vast sections temporarily out of tune with middle-class life. Here in pop cultureland lay the idea of youth as a new kind of social class: of the kids of the sixties as a generation apart, with a life and heroes of their own.

By 1964, as mods and rockers hit the headlines, the images of British youth had successfully converged, and suddenly a general picture of dissenting youth was presented to a stunned public. In the celebrated Whitsun riots of 1964, in Margate and the other coastal resorts, Youth-in-General had threatened the Sacred British Family Holiday, and in the kangaroo courts following the skirmishes GS scooters and teenage promiscuity suddenly assumed political dimensions. In the eyes of the Margate magistrate the images of

23

Jagger, clean-cut mods *et al.* were inextricably mixed up: 'It is not likely that the air of this town has ever been polluted by hordes of hooligans, male and female, such as we have seen this weekend. These long-haired, unkempt, mentally unstable petty little hoodlums, these are the sawdust Caesars who act like rats and hunt in packs. In so far as this court had been given power, we shall discourage you and other thugs of your kind who are infected with this vicious virus.'

The Whitsun riots took many 'youth experts' by surprise. In the continuing phoney debate on the youth problem, it had even been proclaimed that, with the disappearance of the teds and the rise of beat music, working-class kids had mysteriously cured themselves of gang violence and purged 'juvenile delinquents' from their midst in favour of gentle lead guitarists and cute-looking vocalists. Police officers in Liverpool were ready to testify that pop groups were putting an end to vicious teen gangs. Working-class subcultures in general were thought to be disappearing. The myth of youth as a new social class helped mask the realities and sustain these illusions.

The new *déclassé* milieu of youth that had grown up around the pop scene of the middle sixties was premised, as I have said, on the rejection of the middle-class prefect system and also on the traditional working-class apprenticeship system. The reverberations of these rejections went far beyond the youth ghettos. In the pseudo-egalitarian technocracy of Harold Wilson's Britain of 1964 class distinction was officially considered out of date, and old-school-tie privilege was criticized for being an inefficient and outmoded way of running British industry. The whole of British society was infected by images of youthfulness and modernity: priests, politicians, and parents were fuddy-duddies and urged to 'get with it'.

News had filtered down to the new world that the hoary, tradition-bound heart of the Empire had undergone some mysterious rejuvenation. Swinging London! David Hockney, himself one of Britain's new exportable mod heroes, pointed out that London compared with New York was about as lively as Bradford on a Sunday night, Still, the image was a shot in the arm for the tourist industry, vital to Wilson's balance of payments crisis.

The times were ripe for the coming together of a new counter-ideology for youth, but a counter-ideology with its own prefect system and its own apprenticeship schemes: the world of the hippies and the underground, high point of the middle-class youth culture.

From its beginning in 1966 the hippie scene had a much more extravagant and mythic presentation than anything seen previously; it saw itself consciously as a resistance campaign organized beneath the foundations of the whole of society, which it regarded as built on lies, and it proclaimed that it would blow it up high with love. The beautiful people opposed their cultural parent with the ideology of love; not the traditional bourgeois version of romantic love, but a deliberately disruptive, Americanized, libertarian love which was talked about and above all sung about as the final statement to which there could be no countering action.

The Flower Power cult of 1967 (imported from the USA) was intended as a tactic to smother opposition to its revolutionary myths. The police need not be resisted; they could be given flowers and loved out of existence. The basis of Flower Power, as preached by the official organs of the underground, was individual spontaneity and freedom from restraint. From now on, kids were free to indulge their narcissistic impulses in clothes, speech and manner, as far as they possibly could.

The widely publicized use of cannabis and LSD was more than a convenient challenge to the standards, morals and life-style of the other generation. The obsessive attention of the police, the media and the social research industry ensured drug use as the exclusive public symbol of the hippie.

Allegations of police 'planting' of cannabis in order to abuse the Dangerous Drugs Act were common from 1966 onwards. In December 1966 the fuzz busted John Hopkins, an underground luminary, for possession; the newspaper he had helped to found, *International Times*, main organ of the underground, promptly ran a 'Free Hoppy' campaign, presenting him as a martyr in the generation war over drugs.

In February 1967 *IT*'s offices in Central London were themselves raided, and a whole issue of the newspaper was seized. All over London its readers were subjected to police harassment and malicious provocation. It was obvious, too, even to the other *Times*, that the sentence of three months passed on Mick Jagger for possessing four mild stimulant tablets, legally acquired in Italy, was intended to be exemplary, and was only so harsh because Jagger was a subculture hero. 'It was the verdict of one generation on another,' said *IT*. Almost everyone agreed, including *The Times*.

The generation conflict, seen at its most explicit over drugs, provided the hippie scene with its politics. Proclaimed Yippie leader Jerry Rubin, 'After all, it is a generational revolution we're fighting. A revolution of the youth. And it's international.'

However, the representation of generation conflict as the magical unifier of all under the age of thirty obscured the serious contradictions that existed both within hippiedom itself and with the mass of working-class kids outside who could find little in common with it, and who may only have encountered it through its representations in the Youth Spectacle (unless they lived near a hippie enclave).

The organized expressions of the underground, principally its alternative press, existed in marked contrast to the unofficial coalitions of drop-out youth in the city centres. The official underground had its basis in the avant-gardism and resourcefulness of educated, middle-class hedonists. Uneducated or working-class drop-outs could find a niche in so far as they could exploit specific skills often acquired in the traditional apprenticeship schemes of their class. Carpenters, electricians, painters and builders found a niche as *servicers* to the scene (along with art students who were obviously in demand). These servicers naturally flourished in the *laissez-faire* economic conditions of the alternative society. The late sixties saw the rise of the hippie entrepreneurs: craft shopkeepers, woodworkers, dealers (in clothes, drugs or health foods), restaurateurs, and hustling, self-organizing 'heads'. These were the modern equivalents of the late nineteenth-century petty-bourgeois businessmen.

However, working-class drop-outs who aspired to hippiedom by taking pot, dressing appropriately and hanging out at UFO's (Unlimited Freak-Outs, alternative discos), but lacked the specific skills to qualify as servicers to the scene, existed in a kind of limboland. They lacked the inbred bourgeois gentility which made for real hippies, yet at the same time they had burnt their boats and lost all claim to belong to their own culture. Ironically these were the casualties of the movement, those for whom drug-taking and criminality were less a form of enlightened experimentation than a desperate act of survival. The real drop-outs who came to London from the provinces, and particularly from Glasgow, to bask in the Summer of Love of 1967 were less easy for the 'scene' to cope with, for prominent among them were the *dangerous* classes: violent dope freaks, Borstal Boys on the run and Hell's Angels.

Those underground organizations that were designed for *all* the kids often had a highly contradictory nature. The Arts Labs, which started in London and spread throughout the provinces, were seen primarily as places for all young people to 'do their own thing'. In practice, that meant the 'doers', the cultural avant-gardists, actors, painters, cinéastes, musicians. But the all-welcome sign invited the 'crashers', the real drop-outs, who were largely apathetic to artistic experimentation and mainly concerned with using the Arts Labs as refuges from the ravages of the street, in other words, as homes.

Similarly Release, an underground, anti-drug-bust agency, had a mixed clientele ranging from helpless junkies to rich young Chelseaites who just happened to be raided by over-zealous cops.

These latter elements, children of the *haute-bourgeoisie*, young aristocracy and turned-on professionals – the trendies – had recruited themselves into middle-class-dominated youth terrain for the first time in British history, and sometimes they actually qualified as leaders in hippiedom's upper echelons.

Mick Jagger's 'Playing with Fire', a song about a deb who 'lives with her mother in a block in St John's Wood', and who 'gets her kicks in Stepney not in Knightsbridge anymore', was expressive of this type of parasitism and the underlying parasitism of middle-class youth culture itself, as is this poem by Allan Starr, 'The Afternoon Confessions of Miss Penelope':

> As I cast off the navyblue skirts of school
> I saw daddy's copy of *Time* – Swinging London –
> And I bought a bright red trouser-suit,
> Got a flat in Kensington,
> So good after school, so free:
> Went to the Marquee.
>
> In '67 I got a long-haired boyfriend
> Some beads
> Back copies of *Oz*

> And found that Carnaby Street was just too dead
>     and exploited to bother about.
> Collected lots of memories to tell my grandchildren;
> Minimoke memories of Hyde Park –
> Those were the good days for being young.
> It was love love love to save the world,
> And we believed it at times.

Despite the increasingly stratified, self-conscious and contradictory nature of the hippie scene, and its lack of contact with the outside world, the new prefects, the self-appointed leaders of a generation, saw themselves as classless, controversial and speaking for *all* youth. They were to be challenged by the moral guardians.

The guardians, from the platform of the state and voluntary services – social, educational, police – defended the validity of 'Scouting for the Seventies'; they attacked the evils of drug-taking and sexual experimentation, and were mainly concerned with preventing contamination back at the youth club. Ironically, many maintained a certain class specificity in their arguments; for, although their concern to stop contamination extended to youth in general, their main moral concern was reserved for working youth who might be tempted.

In the sixties we see how the youth problem suffered a massive inflation by the established and alternative media on the one hand, and on the other by the social services and the growing youth-research industry. A badge-festooned *Observer* colour supplement of 1967 babbled on deliriously about the cool liberal rationale behind the alternative society. The liberal establishment defended the new prefects from possible harassment by the illiberal fuzz, and in some cases even employed them to 'tell it like it is' for the benefit of an awestruck and sympathetic NW1 readership. Meanwhile the *News of the World* whipped up hysteria about hippie dope and sex orgies, headmasters called for compulsory haircuts for their charges, and the youth-research industry was raising the study of drug-taking to the level of a scientific discipline.

Of course, as I have already said, a lot of people, from all parts of the country and from widely contrasting backgrounds, had identified with many of the drop-out life-styles espoused by the new prefects and put out by the underground's own media and its big brothers in the pop and film world. But one need hardly stress that for the vast majority of aspiring 'heads' who read *Oz*, but lived far from the centres of youth power, this identification was mainly imaginary. The rock music scene, for example, had helped create the images of a free existence which only its own stars and heroes, who collected the money, had a chance of living in reality. To try to create the conditions in which *everyone* could lead a better life would have meant getting involved in politics, and that action is precisely what was missing from the images the rock and underground media projected.

To cynical eyes the underground in fact often looked like the advance guard of the establishment: its scouts. 'Is it going to go down in history,' declared one angry contributor to *IT*, 'as nothing more than a group of mental colonialists who opened up new markets for the bosses? The pioneers of permissiveness? *A permissiveness that permits the sale of more and more pure rubbish?*' The writer's fears proved more than justified.

For the great mass of its adherents, hippie trippy-ism may have changed everything in imagination while altering nothing in reality, but there was no denying its potential for commercial exploitation. Its sexual revolution was profitably used by the invasion of *Oh! Calcutta* and countless films, records and magazines. Its campaign for the beautification of youth brought on wave upon wave of parasitic boutiques and young fashion magazines.

The following is the front-cover pledge from the long-defunct *Intro* magazine launched by Odhams Press in September 1967, complete with flowers and a brave new format.

What's all the fuss about Flower Children? It seems that everyone over the age of thirty – particularly the national press, the police and the establishment generally – has had something hard to say about the hippies . . . it seems that any girl who throws off her office clothes on Friday night and puts on a cut-down Indian bedspread is in danger of having herself labelled . . . *Intro*'s countrywide investigation estimated that nine out of ten of them *don't* take drugs, *don't* sleep around and, most important, *don't* harm anyone.

In a society where the five-day typist and the weekend swinger were commercially packaged and exploited, the establishment made another conquest. Capitalism got hip and became hip capitalism. The means of mass consumption were actually strengthened and given new life by the interventions of hippiedom.

One of the chief distinguishing features of middle-class youth culture was its innate ability to handle media images of itself (this in sharp contrast to working-class subcultures) and its undoubted willingness to see the world in these terms. Its internationalism (again in sharp contrast to working-class kids' highly localized consciousness) had also meant that the process of cultural self-advertisement and regrouping could constantly be renewed by images from abroad, in particular from the United States.

The surfacing of the British students in the magical year of 1968 undoubtedly owed a great deal to the foreign models of students in the vanguard of revolutionary struggle. Before 1968 British students had no place in the Youth Spectacle. The majority of students were squares or straights in the eyes of hippies, while to working-class kids they were swots and softies. They were of little interest to the media. As late as 1964 Professor Musgrove, a noted youth expert, could write: 'The student population of our mid-twentieth-century [British] university constitutes a negligible political force. Its servility ensures modest and comfortable . . . social and economic rewards.'[1]

By 1968, however, British students had discovered that they did have specific grievances: the authoritarian procedures of the university administrations and the power of vice-chancellors, the unsavoury tie-up of academic and military scientific research, and the victimization of militants who tried to expose these scandals.

Outside the universities the role of the media in whipping up hysteria – first the Tories on immigration, then Labour on the students – revealed a sinister convergence in the functioning of the system. The Labour Party, now well settled in its extended term of office, had served notice that it would keep long-recognized freedoms in check. The needs of export competition had provoked a clamping-down on the unions, and the anticipated immobilization of resistance through anti-strike legislation. The control of wages and salaries, it was suggested, might now carry the added threat of police action and gaol.

1. F. Musgrove, *Youth and the Social Order*, Routledge, 1964.

After May 1968 some British students were seriously talking of the contradictions of late capitalist institutions; others conjured visions of Trotskyist revolution, although the majority simply wanted to obtain their degrees – a safe passport in the straight world. Leftist political models were largely borrowed. Tactics and fashionable modes of Marxism were imported by socialist societies up and down the country at the expense of concrete analyses of British society. Some of the leaders of LSE's revolt, for example, were American refugees from the battlefronts of Berkeley and Columbia. Students became political, acting out imagined Guevarist fantasies and the subterranean Vietcong role, reviving the archaic metaphysic of Trotskyism to explain the world capitalist crisis.

The artificiality of British students handling foreign ideologies lent a desperate authoritarianism to their organizing. In the occupations of the London School of Economics, Hornsey College and Essex University, everything looked like Paris under siege; the posters and slogans were on standard Left Bank lines. Liberation was debated but its essence was sadly lacking from these facsimiles of revolt.

In particular, the element of parasitism on the working-class subcultures that can be detected in the middle sixties took a new twist in post-1968 student politics, where it became emulation. Students acted out a whole choreography of the mob, loosely based on British workers in struggle and on the new territorial violence of emergent football Ends. They came out on strike and stormed through the quiet halls of Academe, breaking windows and rules of public order as they went. The factory workers grumbled about the waste of taxpayers' money, sick to death of hearing the word 'socialism' from uninformed ideologues; while back on the terraces the Chelsea Shed greeted their exemplary actions with ribald chants of 'students, students, ha-ha-ha'.

The increase in sheer student numbers (from 2 per cent of their age group before the Second World War to 11 per cent in 1968) and the fact that they came from a much wider social spectrum than ever before may have helped the development of these emulative tendencies. Greater social fluidity tends to ensure the prominence of working-class and lower-middle-class youth in aggressive, anti-authoritarian activities.

Perhaps all this sounds rather harsh and dismissive: I do not wish

31

it to be so. Students at LSE, for example, did succeed in beginning to control their own social space; they began to publicize it and to develop union power. But the unworkable rhetoric of their politics ensured that they existed in a void, as one of the most despised groups of the population, and despite the ways in which at times they emulated street gangs and soccer mobs they were unable to reach and communicate with the youth of the country as a whole.

The tendency to emulation soon spread to other sections of middle-class youth. The lawless occupation of a mansion at 144 Piccadilly in 1969 finally blew the official hippie image of peace and love. Here in the city centre was a youth mob that was less easy to defend. The liberal media, allies of the official underground, threw up their hands in horror at this ugly escapade. Images of lawlessness, anger and violence abounded in the declining underground press where earlier the scent of incense had wafted.

Even the Miss Penelopes of the scene may have recognized in the rise of militant students and soccer skinheads, and the insidious scapegoat-hunting of Wilsonite Britain, the end of the idyll of hippie trippy-ism.

> But the cold winds came
> I realized that no Government ever gives up freely.
> Love love love just wasn't enough.
> We had to come tough.
> The May revolts thrilled me.
> And so I got a starred beret.
> A white headband
> A red flag.
> A psychedelic poster of Che,
> A little red book in the original chinese.
> I pulled the bright red patch from my levis
> And left the hole fraying.
> I stood for hours in grey rainy weather,
> Swayed by the cling of the crowd.

I am not quoting these lines out of cynicism of whiter-than-white purity. From my own area of involvement in the underground press, and later in the student movement of 1968, I was implicated in at least part of the process I have described.

We tried to politicize the mythologies of youth rebellion. What we produced was another political mythology. WE ARE THE SECRET AGENTS OF THE WORKLESS SOCIETY OF THE FUTURE ... WE DON'T GIVE A DAMN FOR YOUR LABELS AND YOUR LIES. WE'RE NOT SELLING ANY ALIBIS. WE ARE THE WRITING ON YOUR WALL ...

Was there a unifying tendency in the various generation struggles of those times? Skinheads, hippies, black youth, students – instead of fighting or trying to emulate each other, was there a common cause?

In the great Vietnam solidarity march of October 1968 bands of Millwall skinhead soccer boys could be seen yapping at the heels of the demonstrators. They were hostile, curious. They came as excluded, unwelcome onlookers to the high-point of the youth revolution. This underlines the real lesson of the time: the Youth Spectacle had had one effect on the working-class kids. The student marches and hippie communes had brought to the surface all the ugly class hatred and resentments that smoulder at the core of our society.

# The Making of a Sixties Mod

In the early sixties the phoney public debate of the youth problem reached absurd heights. But what of its impact on working-class kids?

In the interview that follows Ian Freeman describes how, after failing his eleven-plus and working in a boring job, he embarked on an alternative career on the mod scene in Folkestone in the early sixties. This was not what his parents had in mind but, since a 'realistic' future of 'settling-down' would not have been very different from his parents' present life-style, his escape into mod was also an escape from them. For Ian Freeman and his friends 'stranded in a dead town' the mod cult gave a voice to the gap that had opened up between parents and children. For working-class people this gap had not been created by the notional inevitability of conflict between generations, some innate urge of youth to rebel, but had been brought on by real material changes. What can a father working in a craft industry teach about work when his child enters the deskilled world of a plastics factory? How can a mother pass on accumulated wisdom about household management when she is forced to work five days a week? How can a parent who went to Chapel, Scouts, or Boys' Brigade be expected to understand teenagers' leisure pursuits, or their street life, in order to intervene? Many of this new generation were growing up in literally a different world – in new towns, suburbs and council estates – where experiences and expectations were vastly different from their parents' formative ones.

In Ian Freeman's account the self-reinforcing process of teenage separation into their own social worlds is under way.

'I came from an immigrant family, but they really tried to be British. My mother came from a quite well-off French family, and then came to England and had to work as a char. But she really wanted to teach us her values. We weren't allowed to play with the other kids on our council estate. At school I really tried hard to be better than I actually was. I was really disappointed when I failed my eleven-plus. I ended up going to a secondary school, and I felt common and I felt cheap: common and cheap because I was taught that secondary school was no good – all the other kids off our council estate went there. I was encouraged by mum to keep away from them. So I never really mixed a lot. I was mainly into cycling and spent most of my spare time doing that. I left school in 1964, when I was fourteen, and I started work when I was fifteen in August '64.

'My first job was in a really old-fashioned tailor's and clothing shop. I was getting something like a couple of quid a week, really lousy wages. It was really bad. I had to work in the shop all day long, appearing as if I was busy even if there was nothing to do. I was continually taking boxes down off shelves and dusting them for no reason. It was really shitty work. I worked in this shop for six months and I was quite a model worker. I used to obey everything that was said, and I carried on with my cycling and that was it. It was the first time I had money, but because my family was really poor most of my money went to them.

'After six months I really flipped. I just couldn't see the point of what I was doing, I suppose. I had a mate who used to come into the shop, and we started to rip things off from the stock. We had it all organized, how to rip things off. It was the only way I could get clothes. I never had enough money to buy them.

'One thing my mate and I used to do when no one was looking was throw bundles of clothes out of the window at the back. Or he used to come into the shop with a knapsack filled with paper, and we used to go upstairs into the back room, take the paper out of the rucksack, fill it with clothes and rush out of the shop.

'During this time – the summer of '64 – I started going out in the evenings. I started going to dances in Folkestone. It was quite a "groovy" town at this time. It was one of the first on the South Coast that started getting invaded by bunches of kids from London. It had always been a holiday town, of course, but before this it had been a different class holiday town to, say, Southend, because all the old dears used to go there, as well as better-off people. So it was really a dead town with one or two amusement arcades and nothing much more than that. It hadn't got the lights of Margate or Southend. But now there was this whole new Folkestone scene. There were quite a lot of beat groups based down there. Noel Redding used to play in the local Red Mousse. He played with Jimi Hendrix later on. He [Noel] was a local hero. There weren't beat clubs, as such, in Folkestone. It was more like in the Odeon bar at the local cinema. Then a beat club did open up – a local group called The Sundowners, who got a recording contract at the time of summer '64, when beat groups became *the* burning issue! So we started going to this club and to dances at night. We used to go to dances in the country, in village town halls dotted around Folkestone.

'Because Folkestone was a holiday town there were a lot of cafés, which was quite unusual for such a respectable middle-class town. And we gradually took one of these places over – just me and my mates and different kids from around. It was not one group. A lot of different people started to use that coffee bar. They came from all over, from different class backgrounds, some a lot poorer than me, even. I went into one of these kids' houses once. My family had no money but our place was always clean. This was a real slum. I was horrified. On the other hand, it was the first time I went into a really posh house, where one of the other coffee bar kids came from. So it was really a very mixed scene, and it was also quite a small group. You would always meet the same people – quite exclusive! But there was one very big influence on us from outside, that was some groups of London kids, mainly from Shepherd's Bush and Brixton, who started coming down and using Folkestone, and bringing drugs down.

'*Drugs* – it was speed at the time. Blues and dexedrine – "dexys". There were two types of dexys, single dex and double dex, and you used to pay a shilling for each of 'em. Because I was working in a grotty old clothes shop there was no possibility of me getting some bread together to buy these things, so I started ripping off from the till so I could get some "gear" – that's what we used to call amphetamines. We started buying it off the kids who came down from London. The market was firstly all the people who used the coffee bar, and then mates of theirs.

'In 1965 I got a new job through my mate who was the manager, at sixteen, of the first boutique in Folkestone, called the Modern Male. I was fifteen. To work in the boutique meant a lot of prestige on the scene. Also the woman who owned the place had no real stock-control. So we used to take clothes from the shop.

'The main thing about working in the boutique, though, was it helped me to fit in, to finally be one of the lads. According to my mum the rest of my age group had been either too posh or too common and I was kept away. So now at the boutique I really felt I had made it. It gave me some sense of identity, not just with the lads – with the birds as well, with the "chicks", as we called 'em then. Because the girls knew you could nick 'em a sweater, they used to come and chat you up in the shop. And we could get free or cheap clothes for ourselves.

'It got to be a really big fantasy – dressing just right: huge white polka-dot shirts with ties with black spots, bell-bottom jeans, Beatle boots, boots with heels. We spent hours dressing.

'The difference between the people we used to regard as greasers and us was that the greasers were always called dirty, from messing about with motorbikes, while we were always clean and smart. We would ruin all our nice clothes on one night on pills, though. Fifty French blues or fifty single dexys in one sitting. Really fucked our bodies up.

'There were slightly stronger drugs like black bombers which used to go for one and six or two bob. You could also buy things from the chemist, like inhalers, ephedrine for asthma. We would go in and say, "My grandad's got a weak heart," or "I got asthma." This was before the law turned on to what was going on.

'There was one particular place where we all used to go and that was the High Street – a little cobbled High Street with two coffee bars. One was called Maria's, all the mods went there. The other was the Acropolis, beats and CND types used to go there. They were older, better educated than the mods, in Acropolis. We used to have earnest discussions in Maria's about whether you were a mod or an individualist – someone who didn't wear all the commercial gear mods were supposed to wear. All the fashions were imported, the mod scene was always very commercialized. But you could be an individualist by using very subtle fashion changes that made you stand out from the crowd. Eventually I regarded myself as an individualist. Also, politics. I went to a couple of YCND meetings, but I was also having serious discussions with the Union Movement.[1] Quite a few of us were. A guy who worked in the amusement arcade was a local contact for the Union Movement. We really hated black kids. Not that there were any in Folkestone – a pretty racialist town like all those small South Coast towns. But it shows how confused our heads were about politics. We talked so much, maybe, because sex wasn't a big scene – if you swallow fifty dubes you just can't fuck, you can't get a hard on. So it was more like rapping endlessly and looning around the town all night. Of course the cops started to look out for us at night. There was a very anti-pig feeling among us.

'Some of us had scooters. They went down to Hastings that summer of '64 when all the London mods went down to Hastings. The rest of us would go up to Margate – jumping the train and going up Dreamland, and seeing the Pretty Things, and being pilled out of our heads. Just walking up and down the seafront of Margate all night. There were coffee bars open there till three or four in the morning. And there were occasional parties in houses where parents had gone away. Whole weekends stoned out listening to sound – R 'n' B, blue beat, Georgie Fame – records imported from London. The pill-taking got really competitive; the more you took the more "in" you were.

'By 1965 I was completely involved in the mod scene: working all day, pilled-up all night. I couldn't be a full-time mod and live at home, though; so I moved out. There were a lot of people sleeping on the beach, so I joined 'em. One night I was lying on the beach under these blankets and the pigs turned up and hauled me off for drugs. Being confined in a small cell when you are on pills is not good! You need to move about, and I needed to! I had some bombers on me when they picked me up and the only way of getting rid of 'em was taking 'em, so I was very stoned – and very frightened – in that cell. They tried to interview me but couldn't. I kept falling about all over the place. They weren't even that sure what was wrong with me. Eventually I turned a table over on top of 'em while they were

1. A fascist group led by Sir Oswald Mosley, forerunners of the National Front.

trying to question me. These three coppers got out from under the table and beat the shit out of me. Then they left me in the cell for a day and a half. They eventually found out who my parents were and told them, but they didn't want to know anything about it. I got hauled off to a remand home, Ashford in Kent. I was sixteen.

'In Ashford they cut all my hair. They took all my gear away and put me in a uniform – a green jacket and short trousers – and we used to have to march along the street in crocodile to go to church. There were a lot of mods from South London in Ashford, and also black kids, who I had never met before. I had to see a psychiatrist and take IQ tests, but then my mother said she would have me back and they let me out – put me on probation for three years. For a few months after, I hardly left home to go into town. I put on a lot of weight and had this terrible short haircut. Once I ventured into town and the copper who arrested me saw me getting off the bus and said, "Stay out of town or I'll do you again," and put me on the next bus home.

'But the pull of the scene soon came back. My reputation had increased. I'd moved up the hierarchy and I'd even started going to the hip coffee bar up the road, where they were already doing hash instead of pills. I even got more into fucking, not all night in bed though, more a quick fuck up the back alley. I started using hairspray – our hair was always combed back and slightly to one side with the back bit combed back. I've still got the back bit combed back! Where greasers looked tough, mods were supposed to look soft cos of things like this. But there used to be a lot of mod fights as well. The mods controlled the centre of Folkestone, and they often came up against the soldiers who were stationed near by, and then up against the military police at night. The military hated us and we hated them.

'By the end of '65, part of the scene had gone softer – hash, The Beatles and all that. But part of it had got much harder. There were certain towns by now designated as mod strongholds; others were known as greaser towns, like Ashford and Dover. Some of us started going up Ashford thirty- or forty-strong – there was a good beat club, the 65 Club, up there – and there used to be bad fights between the mods and rockers. The rockers carried chains and broken bottles. We used to carry long thin knives, like a Japanese paper-knife, which

39

fitted into a tube so it looked like a fat pencil. Often we would go and invade towns and the cops would meet us at the edge of town if we were on scooters, or at the station if we came by train, and send us back home. This led to running battles between the cops and mods. We were encouraged by the press hysteria. The *News of the World* showed pictures one week of these discos in Soho, where there were mattresses on the floor, so we all went up there, and to the Flamingo Club where Georgie Fame played. Or if the newspapers reported that the rockers' bike gangs were going to invade the South Coast resorts we would get all excited and ready to meet 'em.

'Looking back now, the scene couldn't have lasted more than three years. By 1966 it had died. The more working-class of the new generation coming up were turning hard mod into skins. The beats in the Acropolis coffee bar in '64 were changing too, and becoming more like hippies.'

Ian Freeman went on to recall how football 'wasn't a big thing among mods, although a lot of London mods went to football. They didn't go to watch with their dads or uncles as they used to. A few of us even started going up to see Folkestone playing in the Southern League. And if they were playing a big team – Crewe was a big team for us – then more of us would go. But we never used to do anything special there. There was no End for the youth then, nothing like that ...

In 1966 England won the World Cup, and football coverage was dramatically increased and spectacularized by the media. The new generation of working-class kids started going in numbers together. These hard mods or skins were eventually to win another social space for youth – this time on the parents' home ground. But this story, of the dramatic prominence given to football by working-class youth, does not start in England but in Glasgow, long-time home of passionate team support and of a volatile and atavistic youth culture.

# At the Gemme

For students of labour history the story of Glasgow is summed up in Red Clydeside, the shop stewards' movement, apprentices' strikes and the lives of men like John McLean. But there are other proletarian traditions which have claimed even wider and more passionate loyalties because they too express social aspirations and conflicts – one is football.

> It's a dear old cup to fight for,
> It's a dear old team to win.
> When you read their history
> It's enough to make your heart growin.
> We don't care whether we win or lose or draw
> Damn the hair we care!
> For we only know that there's goin' to be a match
> And Glasgow Celtic will be there!

Long before soccer hooligans made the headlines Glasgow had been the home of reputedly the most fanatical and sectarian soccer supporters in Europe. When the 'auld firm' – Celtic and Rangers – met, the city divided: Catholic and Protestant. The terraces of Ibrox and Parkhead became Scotland's Belfast.

> Follow, follow,
> We will follow on
> Anyhow, anywhere,
> Glasgow Rangers will be there.

But supporting Rangers or Celtic is only one strand in a wider popular history, that of the gang cultures of Glasgow youth. From the big Protestant and Catholic razor gangs of the thirties, vividly portrayed in the pages of *No Mean City*,[1] to their successors of the

1. Alexander McArthur and H. K. Long, *No Mean City*, Spearman, 1982.

seventies, featured in *A Glasgow Gang Observed*,[2] Glasgow youth have continuously made the headlines, their chroniclers the bestseller lists. Journalists and novelists, pop stars and politicians have all pronounced on Glasgow's problem. Long before skinheads and soccer hooligans became notorious, the picture was built up of Glasgow teenagers involved in unchanging, senseless violence, both on the soccer terraces and in the community.

The real story is perhaps more complicated than that. Gangs and soccer support have been key ways in which successive generations of Glaswegian men have made sense of the material oppression of their everyday lives, as well as of their place in the changing social landscape of the city as a whole. Maryhill, a suburb in the north-west of the city, which had undergone rapid industrialization in the mid nineteenth century, is an example. To man the papermills, shipyards and chemical works, centred on the Forth and Clyde canal and the river Kelvin, a large mixed immigrant population moved to Maryhill: Irish, Highlanders and the poorer classes from the surrounding countryside. Their religious and economic differences provided a basis for a strong and continuing gang culture.

In the 1930s the City Corporation policy of rehousing areas *en masse* meant that gang traditions and patterns of team support were imported intact on to the new estates. The Valley, who were Catholics, had ruled in Maryhill, and now local versions of such a traditional gang could be found throughout the city. These gangs were always adult-dominated and sectarian in character. The most famous of the razor gangs of the thirties, the Billy Boys of Bridgeton, and their rivals, the Tims, were Protestant and Catholic, Rangers and Celtic, respectively.

The Second World War proved a watershed in the history of Glasgow gangs. Those which had been dominated by ultra-violent, professionally criminal family clans began to lose ground. Others, such as the Billy Boys, who were more broadly sectarian in appeal, gained in importance and retained a strong adult membership of 'hard men'. The legend of the 'hard man' originated here. At the same time there was a gradual move towards a more youthful

2. James Patrick, *A Glasgow Gang Observed*, Eyre Methuen, 1973.

membership. But the interests of many of these new recruits began to differ widely from their elders.

In the fifties Glasgow developed its own versions of the national trends in youth culture, its own teddy boys, rockers and the rest, but with an added edge of 'hardness', a more pronounced dependence on violence, hard drinking and the fanatical following of football.

The sixties saw the completion of new mass-housing developments, with their familiar lack of public amenities and their proportionately larger first generation of adolescents. Juvenile street gangs grew in numbers and popularity. And the traditional adult gangs began to be left behind in the slipstream of the mod cult.

The older gangs were usually twenty- to thirty-strong at the core, defending small patches of territory. Each gang had its complement of 'hard men', and membership was firmly based on religion. Mass gangs of mods in the mid-sixties, such as The Fleet, who originated in Maryhill, drew in recruits from all over the city and cut across the religious divide. Territorial infighting diminished. Instead the whole city was regarded as a potential site for invasion. Even Sauchiehall Street was 'taken': it's R'n'B club, The Maryland, became the major Fleet venue, in preference to Parkhead or the Orange clubs. And Fleet leaders not only had to be the best fighters; they also had to be the most prominent style-setters and fashion merchants.

Violence still played an important role in Glasgow mod displays – these were armed teenagers. Virtually every laddie carried a knife – a chib – or a sharpened comb. They were among the first aerosol paint-spray artists. Their graffiti spread their reputation far and wide, to Liverpool, Birmingham, London and beyond. The popular graffiti, – RULES OK, originated in Glasgow and was soon to be copied, particularly by soccer-based mobs of youth down south. They also had their own hierarchies and subdivisions which for the first time allowed children and girls to be in on the action: The Fleet Young Team, The Tiny Fleet, The Scooter Fleet, The Girls' Teams. Widespread defacement of the city landscape – smashed phone boxes, walls covered with aerosol graffiti – was the trademark of these pacesetters in the rules and rituals that were to govern the 'teenage rampage'.

As public alarm increased, so did official attempts at control. Police riot squads and special mobile units, more and better youth clubs, were some of the methods employed by the City Corporation to get the kids off the streets. All this had little effect on older Fleet members, who were already disappearing from the scene, whether through marriage, migration or gaol. But it did serve to break up the younger Teams and led to the re-emergence of small territory-based gangs, only this time more often centred on youth clubs than anything else. The Cadder Young Team, The Barnes Road, The Ruchill Boys, The Fernie, The Young Rolland Boys, The Barracks Young Fleet: often the only time they would all be bound together in a single mob would be on the soccer terrace.

The one facet of the Glasgow mods that survived was the passionate enthusiasm for rock 'n' roll. In the late seventies the city was a leading centre for the emergence of 'new wave' punk bands. They attracted large mixed audiences for whom narrow territorial, not to mention religious, loyalties were more than ever an absurd irrelevance. Today, punk is the dominant youth cult in Glasgow, as in Belfast. But with unemployment well above the national average, many are turning to a yet more individualistic and negative solution: drug-taking – from glue-sniffing to heroin addiction, which is increasing rapidly.[3] Some users are as young as twelve and thirteen, so that Glasgow is well on the way to becoming a major heroin centre.

The Billy Boys are still around, though. And so, of course, are Rangers and Celtic and the social clubs they sponsor. Attendances may have dropped but the 'auld firm' still dominates the Scottish League, and full-grown men, some in their fifties, can be observed fighting and leading the charge on rival fans following a Rangers–Celtic clash. Colin Clarke comes from Easterhouse district and was one of the first young people to dare to walk the streets dressed as a punk. Like many of his generation he sees only pathos and futility in the faces of Glasgow soccer fans.

In January 1968, sixty Glasgow Rangers supporters lost their lives after a crash-barrier collapsed on the terrace at Ibrox Park. In Glasgow I was told that 'Some sick Fenians [Catholics] called it

3. According to a research report there were an estimated thousand young heroin addicts alone. See 'Rapid Increase in Heroin Addiction in Glasgow in 1981', Glasgow University, 1981.

the Orange Crush.' In London a Stepney schoolboy, Peter Kett,
wrote his own epitaph to the dead fans.

### The Ibrox Disaster

It was Hogmanay
When everybody doesn't go to work
   for a week,
They just get drunk.
They fight, till they fall.
Then came the climax of the week –
RANGERS *v.* CELTIC,
The two best teams in Scotland.
All was well at half-time,
RANGERS 0 CELTIC 0,
The fans were happy
And drunk.
Then one minute from time
A Celtic attack built up,
A shot from a Celtic player
Crashed against the cross-bar,
Then as the ball rebounded into play
   with the goalkeeper helpless,
A Celtic player called Jimmy Johnstone
   headed it into the net.
Then the whole stadium exploded,
The Celtic fans went mad,
Certain for victory,
The Rangers fans started to go home
With thinking of defeat.
Then as the crowd moved away
With ten seconds to go,
Rangers scored with a free kick
   from Colin Stein.
The Rangers fans that were leaving
   heard a roar.
Then a little boy who was leaving the stadium
Ran up to the top of the steps –
'They've scored, Rangers have scored.'
As he turned round
He pulled his coat over his head
And fell back down the steps.

## We Hate Humans

As he struggled to get up
The Rangers fans tried to get back to see,
But then it happened
So quick
People toppling over
Just like that.
A barrier broke –
People
Squashed, crushed, suffocated to death
Just like that.
As they laid the bodies on the pitch
It looked more like a cemetery . . .

# Born on the North Bank

I was born on the North Bank
Balls are made for kicking
When you go down the North Bank
Knives are made for sticking.

Highbury skinhead song

During the middle sixties the 'hard mod' image of the Glasgow gangs spread south. And that included the tradition of ardent, passionate support for football. Away-match travellers with the successful Liverpool team[1] set the standard – the Liverpool Kop's stunning arrangements of popular songs, such as 'You'll never walk alone' (or Again), became rich sources of emulation. They rolled up their jeans the better to reveal their Doctor Marten industrial boots, wore braces, cropped their hair – got known as suedeheads, skinheads. They went to football *en masse* and took over the terraces in a way that previous generations had never done. They excluded the older supporters and took the names of the terraces they controlled as their own.

Stuart Pane, a trainee messenger-boy with the Post Office, was eighteen when I interviewed him. He had been one of the several thousand teenagers who joined in this long march, from the North Banks of London, from the Liverpool Kop, the length and breadth of the country, from Glasgow right down to the seafront of Southend.

'I was about seven years old. I played for the school team – Grange Park – where I lived. So once I started playing football, in the breaks and then for the school, I got interested in it. I wanted to go and see proper games like, with the professionals playing football. The first time I went, I went down Tottenham and I thought, "That's a load of rubbish, I wouldn't go down there no more." So I went up Arsenal a couple of times. They were no better.

'This was when Tottenham just come out of their great run when

1. On Merseyside strong traditions of sectarian rivalry existed between Liverpool (Protestant) and Everton (Catholic), as in Glasgow. In the middle sixties the Kop not only still sang sectarian battle hymns but also selections from the Mersey Sound.

they won the double, and Arsenal, they was under Billy Wright then.
But it didn't really interest me to watch 'em play. You look to learn
things from the game, right? But it weren't interesting enough. So
then I left it out, you know. I just played for the school up to when
I was eleven, when I left school.

'And me nan she moved to Rayleigh, near Southend, and I went
down there in the summer holidays, six weeks' summer holiday, and
that was right opposite a park, and I used to go over there like,
to play football. And this bloke come out, and he said, "D'you wanna
play for us? We got a team, you know, Rayleigh Athletic. Do you
wanna play for 'em?" So I goes, "Yeah, all right." So I played for
'em and another team called Ferndale. So I played over there.

'And then me big brother, I dunno, he must have been about
sixteen then, he goes, "Come down Southend, see the football." He
was going with some of his mates, and me cousin lives down there,
so there was about eight or ten of us went down there, watched
the game.

'I thought it was good, you know; it was exciting. They was in
the Fourth Division then. The defences are weaker, they don't play
so much tactics. In the First Division they just put out tactics to
stop certain players. But out there you just put eleven against eleven
and you play it out. So it was more interesting. The first game we
see was 4–2 at Southend. All the scores was big. It was interesting
cos there was a lot of goals, and it was exciting cos of the weak
defences. So I went down there a lot. Then, when I was thirteen,
it wasn't just the football – I started going down there with crew-cut
and boots. Thought I was a right little lad, thought I was a hard
nut. All I knew at the time was the kids with the boots just sang.
You went up there, on the North Bank, and you sang in a little
group like; you kept it in the group. That's all I thought about it
at first. Then I realized the idea's like to keep your End and fight
off all the others. All the big kids going, "Ah, let's have that geezer
over there," and all this. They must have been about seventeen to
twenty, really big, hard-looking geezers. I was thirteen. There was
one bloke, Ginger, he had a white butcher's coat with SOUTHEND
on the back. Then you started walkin' around after 'em, like a little
lad.

'But I dunno how it started, trying to chase the others out. To me it just happened. One week you just went to see the game, the next week you were going there to have a good kickin'. That was it. Fuckin', I dunno how it started. I dunno who got hold of it. I suppose someone nicked another kid's scarf and it started from there.

'I waited till I was fourteen, fifteen, then I started going to the away matches. I couldn't pay the train fare. It was too much. Three quid return for a kid. To go up Grimsby, Newport, Doncaster, places like that. So we used to bunk off the trains, sneak in at King's Cross, Paddington, Euston, all them places. When they opened the gates we just used to walk in round the side where the trollies used to go. We used to get on the train. When the ticket blokes come round, we used to threaten 'em or jump in the loo and hide. And at the other end we just used to run through, like, or climb over the fences or whatever there was.

'Cos, money – me old man used to give us a fiver a week. I used to earn some money going over the golf course, caddying like, for the snobs. But it was still too much. Who can afford it? The train fares *and* getting in to the ground. So there never used to be a lot of Southend supporters at away matches. It was fuckin' miles. So we used to just go away and have a laugh. Drinkin' cans of beer. You'd only have about three and you was half pissed.

'Southend, it's not like any other football team. Well, there's a few teams maybe – Brighton, Bournemouth – it's cos it's on the sea coast. If you come from like Newcastle, and you come down to see Newcastle *v.* Tottenham, you only come down for the match. Then you get on the train and go home. That's it. Southend, you come down, see the match, go down the seafront. There's all the discos down there. It's like a day out. There was a mate of mine, Mick. He's moved now. We used to go down there every week. We used to leave early. Get there about ten or eleven, go down the seafront like, for a laugh. See if there was any of the other team, you know, Newport, Doncaster, whoever it was. We used to go and try and give them a kickin', nick their scarves, that was the thing. Then after that we used to go in the pub when it was about twelve o'clock, come out about half past two. There's about four pubs right by the ground. We used to go down the ground, stand up the End and see who was there. I mean, if there was hardly any of the other supporters – and a few times nothin' come down, you couldn't see no one from the other team – then we just use to fuck about. But if there was a few of 'em, we'd climb over the fences, run round the other End, roll the coppers, try and get hold of 'em like. Half the time you'd get around there, look behind yer, and there's only about four kids with yer and about thirty of them like. You think to yourself, Fuckin', what am I doing over here?

'You got different teams pulled more blokes out – hard nuts, looking for a bit of aggro. Any time one of the London teams come down, or Brighton, that was the other one that always used to come down, well if they come down then there used to be a right lot of aggro, a lot of kids come down, like. If it was just a normal game, I dunno, I suppose there'd be about fifty or a hundred [of us].

'Southend, last year, the away support was a bit better than it was. We took a lot up Watford. They wouldn't let us up their End or we would have had 'em. They've got these fuckin' big metal gates with spikes on 'em. We was trying to get over but there was all coppers there, with dogs, you know. We couldn't get over.

'Everyone thinks the Third Division is just a handful of supporters. You've only gotta go and ask a QPR supporter or a Chelsea supporter, they'll tell you how many Southend there are. Chelsea come down in the League Cup, they all got a kickin', they all run out, before half-time, before even a goal was scored like.

'At Southend no one goes down the other End at the start. At the start everyone's up the Southend North Bank. And you see it, it's packed tight. Ask anyone who's gone down there to see a decent team come down. You see it packed tight right the way across. There's hundreds of kids down there cos there ain't no other football team, right out there. When you see where the others [supporters] are going – you got four stands, haven't yer, round a football pitch? – then you're climbin' over walls and fences to have a go at 'em.

'I dunno how it started. There was just growing violence, you know. Really it all started when the coloureds come over here. I mean to me I don't care about 'em. I got a couple of mates wot are coloured geezers. They're all right, you know. A lot of 'em, they're all mouth and they try kung fu and all this. They're bleedin' useless to me, like. But once they started to come over and you started going Paki bashin', nigger bashin' and all this sort of thing, that's what brought the violence up in this country.

'When I was at school, when I was about eight or nine, you never heard of a coloured geezer, know what I mean? If there was a coloured geezer in school, you'd think, Ooh, look at that, a black man! You don't realize it, you know. But when they started comin' over a lot, people started thinking that the white people was going homeless and poor, and the coloured geezers was making a bomb. A bloke who's poor has only gotta see a coloured geezer in a big flash car and he thinks ... To me it don't make a lot of difference. I can't understand how people can say, "I hate black geezers cos they're black." To me, everyone's got their own mind and a way of thinkin'. To some people it don't matter if they're white, pink, yellow, orange. To some people it don't matter, does it? It's how they are. If a bloke's a decent bloke and you get on with him, it don't matter if he's black, if he's a mate. As I said, I got a couple of black mates. And there's some white geezers that come round me that I really hate. Any time I get a chance I have a bundle with 'em. So you can't say that just because they come from Jamaica they're bad. To me they're all right.

'When QPR come down there were so many Southend coppers there. And they're the hardest. No copper's as hard as the Southend copper. They get more money cos it's a private Corporation; it ain't Metropolitan Police or that. And they're right hard bastards. You don't see no little geezers. They're all big meaty blokes.

'They took us down the station when Bristol Rovers come down. I threw a bottle, me mate he threw a can. It was full up with beer. Cut a geezer's head open. I dunno where the bottle went, I just fuckin' threw it. And the coppers come down and they grabbed us out and took us down the station. When you go in, it's like a pay counter at a shop. There's a bloke sitting behind there and he goes, "Right, empty out your pockets," in case you got a knife or something like this. You take out your fags, your money, your comb, whatever you got. You take that out and instead of the copper saying to you, "Come down this room here," he fuckin' hits you one and goes, "Go on, get down there", like. And we was coming down these little steps, about four steps down there. We come down these steps and he tried to push us down these steps; he tried to push us, you know. I turned round on him, right! They don't hit you in the face. If they hit you in the face and you take 'em to court, you got all the marks on your face to prove it. He hit me right in the stomach. Fuckin', I was doubled up. I was lying on the floor.

'It's not until you're older and you look back on it that you see how stupid it is. I mean now, right, I ain't grown out of it cos I still go down there, for a bit of a knuckle ... When I think back, when I was thirteen, think what I used to do, you'd really laugh. Stupid, really, but that's how it goes. You gotta learn. That's how you learn.'

# In the Blood

The generation of school-leavers that emerged in the early seventies was more cut off than any of its predecessors from occupational or other traditions previously passed down through the family and community. This was the combined effect of the urban redevelopments and changes in patterns of employment of the sixties. But where material conditions would allow, traditional ways survived, and team support, like political allegiance or religion, would still get handed down from father to son. In 1977 Stephen James, aged twenty-one, lived and worked on the Bournville estate, Birmingham, alongside his father. 'I'll stand in the same place and support Wolves till I get too old to stand, like my dad. Then I'll go in the seats.' One foot firmly in the soccer culture of his elders; the other sporting a more contemporary bovver boot, however.

'When we were nippers our old man used to take us down to Wolves, cos he supported 'em all his life. The Blues [Birmingham City F C] and the Villa were down the bottom of Division Two then, and Wolves were at the top. We [his sons] have followed 'em ever since – through thick *and* thin. Our dad, he dropped off going when we were about thirteen or fourteen. He disliked the violence. We live in a different society from my dad's when he was a lad.

'Now we go up the North Bank End or, if you get a few away fans coming up, the South Bank End. We stand about halfway down, just under the shelter, always the same spot. We've been doing it for five or six years. At work, at Cadbury's, we talk about it all day long. If we lose to, say, Birmingham, no one speaks to each other on a Monday morning.

'I never have trouble with the Law as a rule. But I've been in trouble with 'em more than once through football. They'll never find a way to stop it. No matter how hard they try, they can't stop it in the streets after the game, or even before the game. The other mobs, they roll up in cars or they come off the trains with a police escort. The mobs who come in the cars, they can roam around Wolverhampton for hours on end without the coppers knowing they're there. You gotta stop 'em. You do it as part of the pride of the club. If your side's doing no good, you gotta win summat. [Laughs.]

'We were up at Blackpool. It's split down the middle, their End is. One half for their fans, one half for the visitors. They started bungin' bricks over at us, and we were bungin' 'em back. Then they were bungin' ten-pence pieces, and we were pickin' 'em up and puttin' 'em in our pockets. At half-time we went down the back of the stand, filled our pockets with bricks, and started bungin' 'em. When the coppers started movin' in, everyone started bungin' at the coppers at the front. My brother, he said to me, "Have a go at their goalie when he comes back up this end." We were right at the back and it was a shot in a million. It got their goalie on the back of the arm. Then everyone started bungin' at 'im then. The ref took the sides off the pitch for ten minutes.

'I got caught for it. Some copper seen me do it and I got caught for it. He pushed everyone out of the way and grabbed me on the shoulder. I said, "Who the hell are you, grabbin' me?" And it weren't no soft grab either. It dug into me skin. I thought, God blimey I've been caught. What shall I tell the old man when I get home? Then against Millwall, at our place [Molyneux], I got caught again for throwin' rocks at some Millwall supporters. They brought me home in a cop car about nine o'clock at night from Wolverhampton to the doorstep, like. "Does so-and-so live here?" "Yes he does." "You the father of this lad?" "What's he done?" I tell you I almost got killed for it. The game? I can't miss it now. I've been going for too long. Cricket? It's so boring, you're bored to tears. Rugby? Too slow. It's got no appeal for me. It's cos football's in my blood and it always will be. The Wolves!'

# Frankie

In the late sixties and early seventies the Ends were not only gathering places for young soccer fans. They also acted as major focal points for street-based skinhead gangs, local crews as well as out-of-town and provincial boys. At big Ends, like Arsenal or West Ham United, a comprehensive coalition of disparate crews would form the backbone of the soccer mob. Frankie Rice, aged sixteen, was a prominent member of one such fighting-crew, the Kington. Based around the Kington estate in North London on weekdays, Saturdays would find them converging on the Arsenal ground and its North Bank terrace.

Unlike Stuart Pane or Stephen James or the majority of lads who wore the same scarves, Frankie was only theoretically a soccer fan. He was only superficially interested in Arsenal and its players, and was almost completely ignorant about other teams. But what really distinguished Frankie from most fans and the rest of 'the Arsenal' was that he was well-known to the police for activities quite apart from his escapades on a Saturday afternoon. At the time I talked with him, he was on probation for taking and driving away a car, compared with which a more recent arrest for assault outside White Hart Lane football ground was a minor offence. Local police officers I spoke to estimated that out of some five hundred hard-core supporters, only about fifty, some 10 per cent, would be known to them in this way. Frankie's record at school and lately at work was little better. He had no educational qualifications, was in fact barely literate, and in the twelve months since leaving school he had held a succession of menial 'crap jobs' and was lately unemployed.

Yet Frankie is neither more nor less typical of the 'hardened juvenile offenders' that the experiments of all the egalitarian social orders in the post-war world, East and West, have unfailingly produced. Delinquent youth has in fact been one of the first side-effects of the 'new urbanism'; of the disintegration of traditional moral codes of behaviour; of the fragmentation of established patterns of working-class ways of living; of the extension of an increasingly barren consumer leisure; of the growing control of every aspect of daily life by the 'benevolent' interventions of agencies of social control, from police to teachers and social workers; and of the economic survival of a family unit that has lost much of its moral significance. Sociologists such as Philip Slater[1] and Richard Sennett[2] have pointed out the inward-looking stifling nature of the post-war family. The child's drift into delinquency means that the family unit is not only isolated from without but undermined from within. But in the gangs and youth ghettos thus created, the inmates are similarly isolated and undermined. The 'juvenile offender' exists as the most powerless element in society, condemned to fight a succession of losing battles against the Law. Frankie Rice's obsession with fighting and territorial violence reflects his perhaps fatal fascination with nihilistic and fatalistic life options. Being a hard nut up the End can never pay the rent. Street crime is the least secure way of obtaining a living wage.

Of course the punk on the street may be trying for a real freedom in the use of his time, even if it is only the freedom to hang around and do nothing. Or he may be trying for an individual assertiveness in his bizarre dress and aggressive behaviour. And up on the soccer terraces he does help to construct a rough community of his own, albeit made up almost entirely of people of his own age, sex and background. But the contradiction of living entirely in and for the juvenile ghetto remains. On the soccer terrace, as elsewhere, the youth mob develops its own hierarchy which can only fulfil itself in wars with other mobs, isolating each group and each individual in the group.

'There was about fifty of us. Some of us went to Islington Green School. There was racial wars there and everything. We used to get all the niggers. There was stabbings in the playground. The teachers, they didn't know what to do about it. We never used to take no notice of them, anyway. So what could they do? And then you've

1. Philip Slater, *The Pursuit of Loneliness*, Penguin, 1975.
2. Richard Sennett, *The Fall of Public Man*, Knopf, 1977.

got them new teachers comin' in now and they think they know it, but they don't. It's just what they read in books. When we was thirteen, fourteen, we used to just go in to school, get signed on and then bunk off. Half the time they [the teachers] never used to bother. It was a load of crap, school. All we did was fight, and we could do that just as well out of school.

'So we used to bunk off school and hang around in a mob round here, all the kids from the estate, the Kington estate, and any time there was any fights we used to gang up with each other. There used to be an arcade where we used to hang about, near Chapel Street market. We'd go in there and wreck the machines till the Old Bill come along. We used to meet the other mobs there and chase them down the road. It was mainly the Angel mob. We never got on too well with them. It was just that they were Arsenal supporters, so we used to get on all right up the Arsenal. But once we was on their territory we used to have fights cos the Arcades really belonged to them. But we used to go down cos we was right next door to it.

'When they come out of school we would give the little kids a kickin', nick their money, especially the Paki kids, get some money somehow and then go home. We used to do that every day. Then we used to go up against the Lever Street, the Hoxton mob. In the evenings we would go to a club called the Hole in the Wall. We used to sit there talkin' and drinkin' and muckin' about with the girls, and then they [the Hoxton] would come over and start trouble – knock our beers over us or get one of our mates outside and cut one of their arms up, not with knives, with bottles. You couldn't just sit there and watch it all happen, so we used to jump 'em and give 'em a kickin' outside. Anything we could get our hands on we used to hit 'em with. I was about fourteen, fifteen, then.

'This club – the Hole in the Wall – it was in Newmark Road, in our territory. But sometimes we would go up Hoxton and have a fight. We used to throw bottles and bricks at them. But we never used to win there. There was always about twenty or thirty of them against us. Sometimes it was about birds. But usually it was because some of them had given our mates a kickin' up the Arsenal, cos the Hoxton, they are Tottenham supporters. And that was it, really. We always used to have fights with them cos we was all different supporters.

'There was one copper, he was a real bastard. He was called Scotty. He used to walk about with his truncheon in his hand. Some other geezer with glasses, he used to patrol in a car with a truncheon ready on the seat, and every time he used to see us he used to whack us on the back with it.

'And then of course we – the Kington – would go up the Arsenal together. Most Arsenal supporters go down the North Bank. The rest go down the Clock End to get the other supporters. The Kington used to go down the Clock End. The Clock End is always best for the Tottenham cos they always form up there. They never go up the North Bank.

'After the game they used to creep out round the back of the End, so we used to have a crew outside waitin' for them. There's so many crews down the Ends. It's more than just one mob. It's not just all the Highbury ... You got the Highbury waitin' outside one gate, and then, say, the Essex Road or, say, the Chapel Street or the Kington waitin' outside the other exits. We used to get the cunts some way or other. We always used to have two or three crews, and it was the same with the others. We used to have loads of different crews up Arsenal.

'But, say, if we was playin' away, we all get together outside the ground, wait to go out in one big crew and then we all steam out together after the game. The other crews run after us. We wait till they're puffed out and turn round and steam into them. When we play away we get it all sorted out first. So many of us would go in one part of their ground, split up inside and then get together again outside after the game.

'Last season when Tottenham came up Arsenal we missed them. We ran all the way up Finsbury Park and we still missed them. We ran all over ...

'There's this geezer up the End called Buster. He's a fantastic fighter. Fuck that – if he was givin' one of us a kickin' he'd shoot your head off with a shotgun. He used to get us goin' with two or three hundred of us in a fight. He's the top man of all the crews, I reckon. He's the best fighter. He's mad, goes around with a shooter or a cut-throat. Any time there's a fight he has to steam in first. He used to have to fight with the top man of the other End. I haven't seen this, I've just heard about it ... The top geezers in the Kington

58

was a bloke called Micky Spiers, and then there was Stanley Pewter. They was all big blokes. The best fighters. They were a bit older than the other kids. Micky and Stan was mates. They're inside now for somink.

'The older ones round 'ere, about twenty-six, they don't go up Arsenal every game. But if anyone's slaggin' Arsenal off in a pub they jump all over them. They do go to see Arsenal play but they don't get into fights. They leave that to us. They're not interested. Well, they're big geezers, ain't they? They're all sort of relations to us, brothers of the people who are in the crews, and we took it off them. We know they was good fighters and they used to protect Arsenal. Well, if we didn't have a crew up there they [the rival supporters] would wreck the ground. They'd take it apart. They're such idiots, so we have to fight them, don't we? The big geezers, that's where we really got it from. Some of our brothers know blokes in the Big Highbury. If there's any trouble they'll always help us . . . There's this geezer with a shooter, he's about twenty. He used to use choppers, knives, now he uses a shooter if anyone slags Arsenal off! Most of these older geezers, they work for a livin'. But they do a lot of nickin' as well, from work like. But they're not real villains, know what I mean? What they do isn't really nickin'. We do a bit of nickin' now and then. When we're bored we might go and do a couple of empty houses to see what we could find.

'Outside of the football, well, some go to work in the week and after we go to clubs or pubs sometimes. But the weekends are best. That's when there's the football *and* the fights in the evenin', with about ten of us, outside the fish and chip shop. You got to fight to protect yourself. You get a bit of a name and you got to protect it, haven't you? You can't just bottle it and walk away. Then you get really slagged off. There's about ten of us now, like I said. We're all together, all mates from round the flats. We live a little way from each other and we go round and call for each other after work. Then we go and sit in pubs with our birds, drinkin' with them. And then after the pub's finished we go home and they [the girls] all walk in front and we all walk behind. And if we get into fights, then the birds fight with the other birds. They're worse than us! They use bottles as well. They go fuckin' mad . . .

'They're all good fighters in our crew. Well that's the idea, isn't it? There's a few no good, they just hang about with us like. They're not really in it. If a kid's not a good fighter then he don't go about with us and that's that. If we think a geezer's all mouth and not really a good fighter, then we just have a fight with him to show him up. They're the real idiots, the right mouthy ones. They just get a kickin' and that's it.

'We have fights between ourselves, sometimes. If someone annoys someone else, then we have a fight and then we just leave it at that, and we don't fight any more. Other times we have fights, but it's more for a laugh, really. We fight with each other. But not really rough. We just muck about. We never go, you know, mad, like we go with the others. Why fight among ourselves when we got other people to fight?

'Sometimes, if there's a big enough crew, we go up the West End, or down Southend. But it's got to be a fuckin' lot to go down for. Really there's fuck-all down there. Mostly we never leave our area. Only to go to work, if your work is out of the area. Or to nick things.

'Now you see it with the little kids round here. Like we were. Right tough little sods. They are always fightin' ... •

### Hooliganism

Ten little football fans
Making rude signs,
One swore at a policeman
Then there were nine.

Nine little football fans
Stirring up some hate,
One got bottled
And then there were eight.

Eight little football fans
The youngest was eleven,
He smashed up a buffet
And then there were seven.

Seven little football fans
Hitting people with sticks,
One tried to fight alone
Then there were six.

Six little football fans
Playing with a knife,
One got stabbed
And then there were five.

Five little football fans
One fell on the floor,
He got crushed
And then there were four.

Four little football fans
Just like you and me,
One threw a penny at the goalie
Then there were three.

Three little football fans
The other team did boo,
But the fans outnumbered them
Then there were two.

Two little fans
After all was done
One ran on the football pitch
Then there was one.

One little football fan
Glad his team had won,
Argued with some other fans
Then there were none.

Peter Kett

# Bowling-Alley Blues

Oakdale is a few miles from the old city of Portsmouth and is one of the largest overspill housing estates in Britain. Some forty thousand people live there in sprawling rows of low-rise three or four bedroom council accommodation. The only buildings which disturb the skyline are the church and the bowling-alley and leisure centre which dominates the shopping mall. Originally imagined as a 'home for heroes' in the immediate post-war boom, Oakdale developed as something of a working-class ghetto, lacking any definable central place, short on both youth and community provision, and with poor public transport links to the rest of the region. Ownership of a car or motorbike has been a key factor in determining both occupational and recreational patterns. Neighbouring Havant, in contrast, is a middle-class residential area with good amenities and public services.

Oakdale may have struggled into a painful existence, ill-planned and lacking any sense of community. But it has showed one of the highest population growths in the country between 1961 and 1973, consisting largely of young married couples. The working-class stratum was drawn from the declining industrial base of nearby Portsmouth (dockyards, engineering, naval installations); but in the fifties and sixties the local labour market housed on the industrial estate was based on electronics and the newer service-industries, and gave new opportunities to a high proportion of married women and school-leavers. Many firms here were subsidiaries of multinational combines, wage-levels were somewhat lower than the rest of the region, and the workforce was weakly unionized. But everyone was in work and living-standards rose. The other major growth sector in local employment was generated by the influx of administrative and commercial enterprises into the Portsmouth city centre, as a result of office-relocation policies directed at London-based firms.

The gradual decline of Portsmouth FC from the First to the Fourth Division, coupled with the first surge of inflation at the end of the sixties, did little to dent the optimistic mood of this community. Local newspapers were full of the story of one of the first families to settle in Oakdale, who had emigrated to Canada but had now returned, saying how glad they were to be back. And the 'I'm Backing Britain' campaign, where workers donated an hour a week without pay, 'for the good of the country', was launched from this area.

But as the economic recession deepened over the seventies and eighties, this mood has given way to more individualistic and fatalistic responses, especially among the young. Multinational firms are implementing a policy of plant rationalization and closure, resulting in large-scale redundancies. Structural unemployment among school-leavers and married women is higher than the average for the South-East. A fall in real disposable incomes, coupled with rising petrol prices, has resulted in a dramatic decline in car and motorbike ownership. And rigidities in the housing-stock have made it increasingly difficult for the second generation of young couples to set up home. Finally the impact of public expenditure cuts combined with a change in office-location policy has reversed middle-class patterns of migration. The original inducement to move to Havant and a 'shiny new world to which a mortgage is an admission ticket' is beginning to ring increasingly hollow in the ears of both middle-class and working-class inhabitants. One indication of the extent of the crisis is that it is here that the Government pioneered industrial retraining schemes.

Oakdale estate is separated from the rest of Havant borough by a railway line and green belt land. The surrounding neighbourhood comprises mainly privately owned accommodation for professional workers – hence the estate is seen as physically and socially distinct (and provides a favourable environment for students of class difference). Oakdale is not looked upon favourably by its neighbours and can fairly be described as a stigmatized council estate. For example, residents often find it difficult to obtain credit.

*Extracts from a Meeting of a Working Party on Youth Provision for Oakdale, May 1973*

MR STEVENS: Mr Johnson, you have been very successful in the last few years as manager of this bowling-alley. To what do you attribute your success?

MR JOHNSON: I think mainly the schools programme. Youngsters start bowling when at school and we try to give them enough enthusiasm in the game to make them want to carry on after leaving school.

MR STEVENS: How many do carry on?

MR JOHNSON: A very small percentage in actual fact carry on. About 20 per cent of the youngsters who have left school carry on bowling and don't leave, either representing the firm they are now working for or joining another League.

MR STEVENS: The first impression you get as you come into the bowling-alley building is the big sign saying NO LEATHER JACKETS AND NO JEANS. How off-putting is this to young people? Or do they in fact stick to the rules?

MR JOHNSON: It was a very difficult thing to put up. It used to be standard procedure in the company. But I always felt it was very wrong to judge someone by what they wear, so when I came here five years ago I took all the notices down. But unfortunately out of all the people who wear leather jackets and jeans a very, very small minority are the troublemakers, and unfortunately you do have to have this rule just to stop them. In the past, bowling centres in this country have had a terrible name, like soccer grounds now. They were the places where all the layabouts, junkies and drop-outs of society gathered. And unfortunately the people who were running them, all they were interested in was making sure the pinball tables filled up with money. They really weren't interested in the bowling side of it. When bowling started in this country in the early sixties, it was a new thing and everybody wanted to bowl. All sorts of people just poured in all the time, and it didn't seem to matter to anyone who was in the centre. The novelty has now worn off, and if you get husband and wife and two youngsters up to bowl one night and this layabout element is in the centre, they won't come again. So a clean-up campaign had to come. We were getting a really bad name. Now we have reversed this trend, and my company would like to look on their bowling centres as an extension of the community centre, something that is open to everyone who wants to bowl.

MR STEVENS: How did you start this clean-up campaign?

MR JOHNSON: In the old days, when there was any trouble, the manager called the police to remove the people concerned. Once they were put outside the premises the proprietor just wasn't interested. They would not allow police in their bowling centres, you see. We are the complete reverse. If the local police want to walk around here in their uniform, we are not ashamed to have uniformed police in the centre. If we call police in, unlike our predecessors we will make a charge if there is an offence. I think this is the biggest deterrent of all. If you can walk in, cause trouble, and know that you will only be thrown out, that is no deterrent. But if you know there are serious consequences ...

MR STEVENS: Talking to young people, your name crops up quite a bit. They obviously know the score when they come in here.

MR JOHNSON: I probably ban more people in this bowling centre than most centres have got bowlers. A couple of youngsters came in only last night who had been banned about three months ago and asked if they could come back in if they behaved themselves. I'll give them another chance.

MR STEVENS: They know exactly where they stand. If they don't toe the line then they are out, and this works?

MR JOHNSON: I think it works. It's very difficult for youngsters, they say there is nothing to do, but there are some very fine youth clubs on the Dale. I think they need good clubs, sports clubs: tennis, badminton and boxing. I think a boxing club would do very well in Oakdale as they seem to be brought up to fight. All the boys feel they must keep their name up.

MR STEVENS: But you are really the only commercial provision here, except for the odd coffee bar like the Caravello. What other viable commercial proposition do you think could eventually come to the Dale? What about a dance hall? The youngsters are always talking about how they need a dance hall. The sixteen- to twenty-year-olds say that they go down to the Mecca in Portsmouth, spend a fiver a Saturday night and then can't afford to go

65

anywhere else during the week. They seem to want a dance hall locally.

MR JOHNSON: I don't know where you go to speak to your youngsters. If you go to clubs and places like this, then these are the dance fanatics. I think the reason they haven't got a dance hall on the Dale is that for some reason they breed trouble. I don't honestly believe that a dance hall is the essential thing for the youngsters. It's something they might want, obviously, but the most important thing at the moment – as we are so close to the sea – is a swimming-pool.

MR STEVENS: That will be ready next February.

MR JOHNSON: I didn't know. This is marvellous. This is something that with an estate of 44,000 is very essential.

MR STEVENS: Yes, it's being built behind the police station ...

# Magic

Housed in a purpose-built extension to a comprehensive school, Oak Hall youth wing is the most modern youth leisure provision in the Oakdale area. It has been thoughtfully designed – up a small pine staircase to a coffee bar, which overlooks a spacious, well-lit expanse – to be filled by table-tennis tables and pinball machines on regular nights, writhing bodies on disco nights. In the following excerpt from a longer series of group discussions at the centre, four of the club regulars prove perceptive commentators on the local life around them. Although things get clouded over at first with parent-influenced fantasies about neighbours, through the process of collective counsel the group moved towards a more sympathetic and respectful understanding of the kind of 'community' that their parents have been forced to settle for, which they will one day inherit, and reached the solutions that kids improvise for themselves.

KAREN: I've lived here [*in Oakdale*] since I was born.

DEBBIE: And me.

CHUBBY: Sixteen years! [*Laughter.*]

DOUG: I've lived here eleven or twelve years. But I'm not living with the same family. I'm adopted. We was living in Portsmouth – down by the docks. It was a dump compared with where we're living now. But this is a dump compared with where we could be living.

DEBBIE: I would move to Portsmouth – for the night-life. It's better than here. There's nothing here for young people except this youth club which shuts at half past nine.

KAREN: There's nothing after that. Except pubs, if we can get served in pubs. So we go wandering around the streets.

CHUBBY: Round here we're out of all the nightclubs for dancing and that.

DOUG: Yeah, but the south of England isn't known for clubs. All the big clubs are in London or up north.

CHUBBY: I went to Birmingham Thursday with my brother – he's a lorry driver – and that's all we see, nightclubs and that, when you go through Birmingham.

KAREN: It's a horrible place, Birmingham. It's all dirty and smoky. We're luckier than that.

CHUBBY: We're luckier than London.

DEBBIE: The area I live in is better than most of here. The actual road we live in, well, it's a council estate, but it's really *quiet* there, isn't it, Chub?

CHUBBY: Yeah, but where you live everybody seems to know everybody else. They're more friendly.

KAREN: I live in a horrible road. I don't talk to anybody round there because they are horrible and scruffy. Fleabags. Loads of tarts. People who've been married about six times and got about ten kids hanging around. No curtains hanging up. Still manage to get a colour telly! They're so scruffy and dirty, they don't care if they live in shit and muck. They *like* living in it. I couldn't live like that.

DOUG: That's your mum talking. [*Laughter.*]

DEBBIE: Her mum was telling me yesterday. This scruffy woman, lives next door to her, and her mum goes, 'Oh, they want to send her down the Crescent!' Where I live! What a bloody cheek! How many scruffy houses are there down our way? It's just the middle patch, isn't it?

KAREN: Yeah, just the middle patch, by the green, about ten houses. You can smell them from one end to the other. [*Laughter.*]

CHUBBY: Hilton Crescent, that's the worst, that's horrible. We had a family from Hilton Crescent at school. The Booths. And they have not had a haircut ... They've newspapers up at the windows, they have! And corrugated iron where the council is sick of mending them. There's a woman there who's got chicken-wire round her windows cos she's so sick of having them smashed. But in that circle, where Paddy Conway lives, that's all right.

DOUG: Is that bit only different because you know Paddy and he's your mate?

KAREN: Yeah, Paddy says, 'Our bit is all right. It's the middle.'

DEBBIE: And the people in the middle say it's all right because *they* live there. *They* say, 'Oh, they're all snobs down the other end!' You always get one group at one end of a street where the women and the husbands know each other, but they don't know the group at the other end. So it's all, 'We don't know them up there. They don't associate with us. So they must be worse than us.' And the other ones at the other end are thinking the same.

DOUG: You see, we say our bit is all right. Debbie says her end of the street is all right. Paddy says his bit is all right. Most parents round here know nobody else who lives outside their bit of street, unless it's relations. It's ridiculous to say so, but there is no community round here. Havant and the whole surrounding is split into ... it's like gang warfare, no joke. There's the Havant mob, Oakdale, Hayling Boys ...

DEBBIE: Emsworth, West Leigh.

CHUBBY: Southbourne.

KAREN: The Point Seven Boys ...

DOUG: Nobody wants to intermingle with anybody else. The only time they want to is at discos. When the disco is on everyone is friendly. As soon as it finishes everybody changes.

DEBBIE: Like Jekyll and Hyde.

KAREN: Everyone keeps to their own part of the community. We keep to our bit, the Point Seven lot keep to their bit.

DOUG: Trouble starts in this area because people restrict other people from going elsewhere. Whenever anybody else comes up here – to this club – we think they are different. But they are not. They're the same as us. They've got a youth club and we're not allowed in there. So they start making trouble. It goes round in a circle.

DEBBIE: What about when you go to Fratton Park,[1] to watch the football. We are all shouting out 'Oakdale!' And there's the Broomfield and the Southbourne lot, we're all one and the same side.

CHUBBY: And the Bedhampton and the Pompey.

KAREN: And there's two silly cows at the back going 'Cow Plain!' [*Laughter.*] And then they start fighting.

CHUBBY: They don't go to watch the game. They go for a scrap.

---

1. Home of Portsmouth FC.

DEBBIE: But they all shout out 'Portsmouth' together.

DOUG: It's got nothing to do with the football.

CHUBBY: But at a big match . . .

KAREN: Yeah, of course. If there's lots of the other team's supporters come down it's different. We're really all together then.

DEBBIE: Otherwise it's still all 'Oakdale's hard!' 'Pompey Boys are hard!' It's still all different communities. But at a big match we're all a big community then.

CHUBBY: It's magic.

# Youth Club Brains Trust

VICAR: Good evening and welcome to our monthly Brains Trust here at St Ida's. This is the panel and I'll introduce them to you. Ladies first. On my left is Edith, a local housewife who is responsible, as some of you know, for a lot of the playgroups that operate in Oakdale. Sitting next to her is Dave Robins, who is a writer on youth, who has come all the way from London to be here tonight. And lastly on the left-wing out there is a footballer who you probably know better than I do. On the best-arranged panels there's always an empty chair. The reason for this one here on my right is that Inspector Willis from Oakdale police station has just telephoned to say sorry but he's unable to make it. So this is the panel and I have collected questions in advance to save trouble. If any of you want to come back on anything said from up here and say, 'Yes, but,' you are allowed to. But only if you signal first by some *acceptable* sign. Yes, John? You wish to leave the room? Well, be quick about it. The first question ... here it is. And it is this: 'Who will win the FA Cup and why?' Now I'm going to ask the soccer expert on the panel that question first – Edith! Do you know who the teams are Edith, first of all?

EDITH: Fulham is one of them.

VICAR: Yes, good, good.

EDITH: And West Ham.

VICAR: Right!

EDITH: They're both Lon ...

VICAR: Yes, they're both London clubs.

EDITH: I don't know, really, I'll say Fulham.

VICAR: Well, whoever asked that question, Mrs Edith Pont thinks that Fulham will win the Cup. She doesn't say why. Now let's ask our second expert, Phil, what he thinks about this.

FOOTBALLER: My feelings on it are mixed. As a young lad I had the unfortunate experience of being a West Ham supporter, but then I got over it as I got older. And I also played for Fulham not long ago, so my feelings will be mixed. Now in the Cup it's just one game each round, and if you win that game you go on. Fulham have been fortunate, played well on the day, and have got to the Final. If I had to plump for one of the sides I would take Fulham, because they have nothing to lose and everything to gain. And probably out of the two clubs I would prefer Fulham to win it.

VICAR: Thank you, Phil. That's two for Fulham. Personally, my vote goes to West Ham. Perhaps Dave will support me on this. Let's ask him.

ROBINS: I'm glad to hear that Phil wants his old club to win. Perhaps he's thinking of leaving his club and going back there. [*No response from the audience*.]

VICAR: I should say that despite the comments of the panel the team colours of our youth club will continue to be West Ham. Right, on to another question. Incidentally, how many people here in this room are due to leave school this week? John, tell us, how do you view school at the moment?

JOHN [*in audience*]: What?

VICAR: How do you view school?

JOHN: A waste of time.

VICAR: Why's that?

JOHN: Cos I've got nothing ...

VICAR: The school has nothing or you have nothing?

JOHN: I have nothing.

VICAR: Why's that?

JOHN: [*Inaudible reply – laughter from mates around him*.]

VICAR: Tony, at the front here, do you feel the same as John?

TONY: No.

VICAR: How do you feel about it?

TONY: I'm happy to stay on.

VICAR: You are happy to stay. Well done. It seems to me you can't teach people if they don't want to learn. I'm sorry, John, that you are going to be bored the next three months. You can always come round here and I'll find you something to do. OK, back to the next question. And it is: 'What does the panel think of platform heels?' Phil?

FOOTBALLER: Platform heels. What can I say about those? Er ... I
don't dislike them, but when I wear them I look about eighteen
foot. I prefer to see them on women.

VICAR: Does your wife wear them?

FOOTBALLER: Yes.

VICAR: And is she shorter than you?

FOOTBALLER: Only four foot shorter. No, seriously, she is shorter.

VICAR: Right, let's ask Edith what she feels about them.

EDITH: I like them, but they make my legs look fat and I have great
difficulty walking in them. But they can look smart if people would
learn to hold their posture right and walk properly. They can also
be very dangerous as I found out myself.

VICAR: What? You fell over?

EDITH: Not so much fell over as didn't look where I was going.

VICAR: I see. Well, let's ask Dave what he feels about platform heels.

ROBINS: I hate them. They look horrible. When I was a kid we used
to wear winkle-pickers. [*Hostile murmurings in audience.*]

VICAR: I don't know whether any of you in the audience want to
come back on anything that the panel has just said, but I must say
I don't agree with Dave Robins because I found winkle-pickers
most uncomfortable. Feet are very cramped in winkle-pickers,
whereas at least in platform heels they spread out because the
toes are square. They may give you other problems. How many
of you have got platform heels on tonight? Hands up! [*Forest of
hands.*] How many of you have ever fallen over because of them?
[*Hands all go down.*] Fair enough. Enough said ... *Now, then*, the
idea of having a Brains Trust here at St Ida's Church youth club
was first mooted last month, after a train carrying soccer fans from
Portsmouth to Southampton had to be stopped because of quite
serious trouble. Possibly some of you were on that train, and so
the club committee decided to have a Brains Trust, with someone
from the football club, and someone who is a bit of an expert.
So listen carefully to this question: 'What is the cause of football
violence, and how can it be avoided?' I will read that again, because
I wasn't sure that *Keith* was listening. Here it is. 'What is the cause
of football violence?' Dave Robins, can you begin on this one?

ROBIN: The causes? Well, I ... This discussion is the wrong way
round. Why don't we ask some of the people here what they think?

What really goes on? Instead of just branding every one as hooligans ... When the press called Man. United fans 'animals' they chanted back, 'We hate humans!'

VICAR: Well, let's go on to Phil.

FOOTBALLER: Was anyone here on that train? [*Half-hearted raising of hands.*] Some supporters told me that there was about eight or nine kids on that train that caused all the trouble, all the damage, and forced the police to take the train into a siding? Is that right? And locked everybody out, four hundred and fifty of you, and kept you there all afternoon. This small minority caused all the trouble. This violent element, they're the ones you've got to find and root out. I have no idea how you can stop them. I don't think anyone has. Otherwise it would have been done by now. All the publicity has done it no good at all – there's too much. As soon as there's trouble anywhere it ends up in the papers, and they seem to relish it and do it all the more. I think the only way is if the genuine supporters – the four hundred and fifty of you on that train, the true supporters – if you could have sorted it out yourselves, found the nine and handed them over to the police, then you would have saved yourselves an afternoon in the railway siding and you would have seen the match. There's no other solution. I don't think passes to get in the ground will work.

VICAR: Let me add a little something in brackets here. This youth club has been running now for eight years and there's been very little trouble of any kind. A lot of you have told me that you wouldn't come if you thought there was going to be trouble. I've tried to get some of you to go to Point Seven[2] and you won't because you think there might be 'trouble', which is another word, surely, for violence. There is a confidence in the members here that when you come you'll be all right, you trust the people that are running it, and also – I take my hat off to the members of this club – when there has been bother caused by people we don't know, you've all rallied round and said, 'Look, we don't behave like that here.' We had a disco here last month when a girl had a little too much to drink and was messing about. I didn't have

2. A nearby 'drop-in' centre catering for 'unclubbables' – unemployed, truant and other 'problem' children.

to do anything. Three of you, three boys, went over and had a little word with her. [*Laughter.*] Well, I didn't say they were cold sober. [*More laughter.*] It's up to the ordinary members, whether of a club or a football crowd, to take the initiative, and if there is any trouble to sit on it straight away ... Let's ask Edith what she thinks about it all.

EDITH: I don't know much about football violence, except what I see on television or read in the newspapers, which is pretty depressing. But I do think that one of the main causes of vandalism and violence is frustration, and over-excitement. Even in the playgroup which I run, if we allowed it to happen, we would have vandalism and violence occurring with youngsters of four or five! It's only because we keep them occupied with the right kinds of material that we manage to prevent it. Violence can start from babyhood. And it will grow! But I do feel that frustration and over-excitement are the main causes of it. I don't know if I'm right.

VICAR: Speaking as an ordinary housewife, Edith, do you ever er ... feel these pressures yourself?

EDITH: Yes, definitely. And, do you know, I could be jolly violent myself. I'm sure of it. I do get it when I'm frustrated. At home I want to smash, you know, the pictures on the wall at home. Or a pane of glass. But you have got to learn to control it, and it's up to us as adults to show teenagers that they can control if they want to. [*To audience*] If you can't control your violence it's a pretty childish way to act! If you are growing up properly it's one of the first things that you have to learn to do.

VICAR: Could I just ask the boys here, particularly – how many of you are there here who regularly play a game? Football, it's mainly going to be, isn't it? Regularly, I said, and by that I mean every week or every fortnight. How many? [*A few hands are raised.*] Right. Hands down. Now, I'll just say this. I'm thirty-six and I too get very frustrated in my life. I don't think I'm particularly abnormal. But I do find it necessary every week to have some form of physical exercise whereby I can really get rid of my frustrations – what she was talking about. And I do recommend to any of you ... er ... that if you want a quick way of getting rid of it all that you take up a game called squash. You can play a whole game of squash in half an hour and get rid of it all! ... But I must say I'm surprised and actually a wee bit disappointed that so few of the boys here regularly play a game of football. Doesn't that surprise you, Dave?

ROBINS: Well, I ... I ... Football is a pretty violent game. It's a game of great skill but it's also violent ...

FOOTBALLER: I disagree with that. I don't think football is a violent game. You may watch it on the television and see someone fall over or someone get hit. But it doesn't happen like that. You see someone going into a tackle and falling over. That's just a genuine tackle that's come about. There is nothing violent in it. You haven't got anybody walking out there with a knife or anything like that. To me that would be violent – when somebody walks out on the pitch with a knife or a gun ...

VICAR: One of the boys at the back wants to ask a question. Yes, John?

JOHN [*from back of hall*]: My mate went for a trial at Pompey, as a defender, and they told 'im 'If they get by you, chop 'em down ...'

FOOTBALLER: Well, the only thing I can say to that is, he might be telling a little white lie, there. I've been in football since I was twelve; I've been playing professionally since I was fifteen and I've never heard of a club, and I've been at three clubs, that has taught anybody anything that is dirty in the sense of elbowing, kicking, punching or anything like that. In fact they teach you the opposite. Because if you start to concentrate on elbowing or kicking someone, then you can't concentrate on the main thing which is the ball. And if you don't concentrate on that you don't play well and you don't end up playing football either.

VICAR: Would you like to say, Phil, one last word to anyone here, as a player, about how you would like them to behave?

FOOTBALLER: The thing I want to emphasize is: there are times when you might get into a fight. That may be no fault of your own. But, especially when you're in a group, there are times when you can stop the trouble, virtually before it starts. If you are a genuine supporter, and you just want to watch a good game of football, as I'm sure the majority of you here are, then you can kill the people off who give football all the trouble. Not actually kill 'em, just stop 'em.

VICAR: Thank you, Phil. That's fine. Now we've just got time for one more question, so, quickly, here it is: 'What would your reaction be to someone you knew who took drugs?' Edith?

EDITH: I think they should admit it to a person who they feel they can talk to and can trust. They should tell them because half the time they go on taking drugs simply because they want to come off them. I take drugs. I wouldn't be alive now if I didn't take them. I wish to God I didn't have to take them. Believe me, when you're hooked it's hard to come off. It's jolly hard to come off. The drugs I'm on are doing me harm. I know it and the doctors know it, and they're trying to get me off them. And I wish I could. I hope to eventually. I want to come off them but I don't know how ...

VICAR: Well, that's about all we have time for, unfortunately. Could I just say that the only person that I've ever banned from this club was somebody who I found was actually pushing drugs to the other members. Not just marijuana – hard stuff like heroin and cocaine. Dangerous drugs. But I had a word with him and he came to me for advice, and he's off drugs now, thank goodness; and he's married and got a family. So that's a happy ending to that one ...

# Part Two

Sometimes when I am lonely
playing football in the park,
hoping to train myself to be a good player
play for my football team WEST HAM
then England or Cyprus

The only thing that stops us is
The barbed wire everywhere.
There have been about a hundred
balls busted at least. They put the
barbed wire there because the ball
goes over and sometimes smashes
the windows of the sweet shops .

George Georghiou, aged fifteen

# A–Z of the Ends

Styles and customs of young fans vary from ground to ground across the country. Northerners, for example, tend to be attracted to the gaudy soccer shop regalia of stickers and medallions; London fans are more relaxed and sophisticated. Each youth End has its own folklore, demography and reasons for coming together.

ARSENAL At Highbury a combination of urban development, old ethnic loyalties, betterment migration and changes in the job market have determined the population of the North Bank End. The 'exiles' returned from Borehamwood, Basildon, Watford, Stevenage New Town, to join up with their North London counterparts and form the North Bank End. Some have come from even farther afield: North London has a strong Irish presence. 'The Dublin Reds come all the way from Ireland [as well as Camden Town] to stand up the North Bank. Now they've got mostly Irish players.'

ASTON VILLA A similar pattern of End composition to Arsenal's emerges in Birmingham, at Aston Villa's Holte End. 'There's some kids from Marsden Green singing "Marsden Green"; some from Chelmsley Wood singing "Chelmsley Wood". Kids from South Yardley sing "South Yardley". Stechford, Solihull, we all come from different areas around Birmingham. We've only got one thing in common – we're for the Villa.'

BIRMINGHAM CITY 'The leaders of the Ends, they run at the front, and just before they come to the crunch they drop back, so it's the poor mugs behind 'em who get the first chunk o' lead smack in their face. The leaders may be the best fighters but they ain't got the biggest bottle.' At Birmingham City, one of the leaders stands smiling, immaculately dressed, arm-in-arm with his girlfriend, while the fighting rages all around him.

BOLTON WANDERERS The first soccer-war fatality was recorded here. In 1976 a sixteen-year-old boy was stabbed to death behind the main stand.

BRISTOL CITY This was the site of a notorious pitched battle in 1977. 'When Bristol lost to Arsenal they all come out of their End. There's a great big park outside, and they all went there, waiting for the Arsenal supporters, and there must have been about seven thousand Arsenal supporters. Then all the Arsenal come out, and Bristol City just run at Arsenal, and Arsenal run back, and they just went charging forward and all the Bristol scattered all over the place. The police was coming along on motorbikes and horses just knocking anyone over.'

CHELSEA Chelsea is a London super-End. Like the Arsenal North Bank, the Shed pulls in recruits from all over Southern England's working-class suburbs. The children of South London people who migrated to Wales during the steel boom of the early sixties have also returned – the Port Talbot Shed. The Shed is noted for its cockney wit, for instance, its adaptation of the West Ham United club song 'We're Forever Blowing Bubbles'.

> We're forever throwing bottles
> Pretty bottles in the air
> They fly so high
> Nearly touch the sky
> And like West Ham they fade and die.
> Arsenal keep running
> Wolves and Tottenham too
> We're the Chelsea Shedboys
> We'll keep running after you!

CRYSTAL PALACE 'That's where all the bike gangs used to go, the greasers, they all supported the Eagles.'

DERBY COUNTY 'Derby is the ground you hate to visit most. They got no one. They get rubbish. They're soft. There's no fighting there. You don't get 'owt there. They're all lasses. No fighting at all. Same at Middlesbrough. There's only about ten skinheads in the Paddock. That's all there is.' (Leeds fan.)

IPSWICH 'A lot of girls follow Ipswich. They don't fight, but some of 'em go over and deliberately chat up the away fans. Then they take 'em round the corner where the Ipswich boys mug 'em, nick their money and scarves. When Ipswich come up London, or Southampton, Norwich, Plymouth – teams from the country, from out in the sticks – all the London kids sing, "I can't read and I can't write, and I just drive a tractor." Ipswich fans think London kids are all mouth, big 'eads ...'

LEEDS UNITED In the sixties, under the managership of Don Revie, Leeds United rose from Second Division obscurity to become one of the most successful teams in Europe. 'But most people in Leeds only went to matches when they were winning. When they won the League in 1974, you got all those big business blokes buying season-tickets. After that, when the team dropped down the League, we didn't get much of a crowd at all. There are not many real supporters in Leeds. It's not passed down, being a football supporter, like it is in Manchester or Liverpool. It's just passed on *between mates*, not through family. It brings the kids together. There are districts in Leeds like Seacroft and Harehills. So they shout, "Seacroft Boys, we are here!" or "Harehills Boys, we are here!" or "York Boys, we are here!" They're all mixed together in Kop. And there's a lad called Varla. He used to wear golden boots. He sprayed 'em gold so that's how you recognize him.'

LIVERPOOL A unique combination of factors – sixties youth culture (the Mersey Sound), sectarian rivalry, a higher than average level of unemployment, civic pride, class militancy and of course passion for football – produced the Liverpool Kop, the Daddy of the Ends. 'It's not the club, it's not the directors, it's not the players, it's not the great successes, it's not even the great managers we've had like Bill Shankly and Bob Paisley. It's a *tradition*, something on its own. When players or supporters join the club they have to fit into it. When we get a new manager, things might be a little different for a couple of months, but then they will go back to being what they were ... It starts early. A little kid of ten will have the whole Liverpool strip, the red shirt and everything. He's totally dedicated. He may never even have been to Anfield ... People may try to prove that Liverpool is Protestant and Everton is Catholic but that is not so true any more. You do get divided families though, you know: "My sister-in-law is coming round tonight with me brother. I'm not looking forward to it. It's a mixed marriage. She's a Liverpool supporter and he's got a season-ticket for the clay-kickers at Everton!" There used to be less trouble with the Kop because there was older men mixed in with the kids, who would soon sort 'em out if there was trouble. But, then, there's always so many in the Kop, other fans would have to be mad to try and take 'em. The Kop has got younger though; there's more trouble now. There's a kid called Lasker who even starts fighting with his mates just to get arrested by the coppers. And older blokes come from Birkenhead and go to the other End. They don't join in the singing; they remain quiet all through the match. Then they start trouble with the visitors. But at Liverpool it's still more a family game than anything. We are still the best-behaved supporters in the land.'

MANCHESTER CITY 'City care about their fans. We've got a social club which has been voted the best working-man's club in the North of England. Most clubs just take the younger fans for granted; City work to attract theirs. We've got the Junior Blues club for kids. You win their allegiance when they are young and once you have won it very few change. The kids can go down to the ground and meet the players if they're in the Junior Blues. There's a lot of community involvement at City. And the ground is virtually all seated now; no mobs forming up behind the goals.'

MANCHESTER UNITED Old Trafford, 1974: Manchester United were faced with relegation from the First Division; to stay up they had to beat Manchester City. A sports commentator describes the scene:

'There are now at least four to five hundred supporters on the pitch in front of us. They have their banners and their flags, and they're really doing no good at all to the club that they are supposed to follow to all the ends of the earth, they are doing them no good now; and now there's a whole wall of policemen going forward, there must be all of a hundred and fifty policemen, and supporters are

falling down; there's one boy in considerable trouble here in front
and there are boots being flung here, there's kicking going on, there
is mayhem down there on the pitch that's meant so much to football.
A policeman's lost his helmet and he's in some trouble, a policeman
on the floor with three or four supporters on top, and then the wave
of policemen come back again and they try and make some sort
of sanity and sense out of all this carnage, because really it's the
most wicked sight to see anywhere in the world but certainly at a
ground which has meant so much, as I say, to this game. There's
one boy being carried off I see in the arms of a policeman and another,
at least three people being carried off, the St John's Ambulance men
going out to try and make some sense of it all. There are now something like fifty or sixty policemen on the pitch, the crowd beginning
to disperse, but this game has been abandoned, the last that
Manchester United will play in the First Division, certainly for one
season, with the local club Manchester City. That's it then, that's
the final scene at Old Trafford, a scene really of destruction and
viciousness, a scene that one doesn't want to see repeated. From
us all at Old Trafford, good-bye.'

'We went down into the Second Division, cos all the other teams
pushed us down, the greatest team in the land. But we come back.
Won the Cup. Stretford Reds will never die! They'll never ban
United!' At its height in the mid-seventies the 25,000 strong Stretford
End was generally agreed by players, managers, police and television
commentators alike to be the most fearsome sight in football.
Manchester City may have had more support in Manchester itself,
but the Stretford was a new phenomenon – a non-territory-based
mob, with nationwide connections from the cockney Reds and the
Tartans of Belfast to branches as far away from Manchester as Deal
and Dover in Kent. The Stretford regularly picked up junior and
senior tearaway elements from the disparate fighting-crews in the
cities they invaded. If you were out of work, a school failure, with
little to do and nowhere to go in your area, there was great appeal
in joining up with the Red army. Before increased travel restrictions
and massive police surveillance were to put an end to their worst
excesses, the Stretford was as proud of its reputation of including
the 'best fighters in the land – killers. We hate humans!' as it was
of following a world-famous team. Meanwhile a new myth took

its place among the many surrounding the origins of how soccer warfare began. 'It was Man. United started it off when they burnt down Norwich's stand . . .'

NEWCASTLE UNITED 'You usually find it's a dim bitch that's got all the bottle. At Newcastle there's a load of skinheads with black and white stripes [the team colours] in their hair, and big beer-bellies. They look like the one in the film *Clockwork Orange*, he was called Dim and he had all the bottle.'

QUEENS PARK RANGERS A distinguishing feature of football in London is the number of professional neighbourhood teams – Orient, Millwall, Brentford. For all the talents and ambitions of its managers and directors, QPR is one such small urban village-eleven, 'the pride of Shepherd's Bush'. It has a built-in regular support of some 10,000, drawn from the surrounding White City estate. Compared with the London super-Ends, the Loft at QPR is numerically weak. 'Twenty Arsenal supporters walked in the Loft one day, and they all run away. They can't hold their own ground. A couple of Second Division teams could take them easy.' So team-ups with rival big Ends are negotiated. 'Say you get QPR *v*. Arsenal and Arsenal take us, and then a couple of months after it's Chelsea–Arsenal. Then you will get all the Loft going with the Shed. All of them drinking together and everything. The Arsenal will be out of it. They will probably have another little End with 'em, like Millwall. And Chelsea joined up with Fulham one time, didn't they? That's cos they all live near each other [in West London]. In London it's like that. Down West Ham, there were Orient with West Ham.' But End alliances are not only confined to close neighbours. As the fans roam the country, word spreads in bars and British Rail buffet cars, of potential, if unlikely, alliances. 'Kids in Leeds think that when they go down London, Millwall will join up with 'em. That's what they *think* anyway.'

TOTTENHAM HOTSPUR To the young fans of Queens Park Ranger, Q+P+R = magic; to their rivals, they are a 'Quarter-Pound of Rubbish'. As for Tottenham Hotspur, they are known simply as 'the yids'. This label originated in the East End, up on

West Ham's North Bank. 'It's cos nearly all the Jews support 'em. There's loads of Jews go up Tottenham.' Traditionally Spurs have always had a strong Jewish following, but on the terraces the word 'Jew' is synonymous with rich, and ever since the double-winning days of the early 1960s the club has projected a rich and glamorous image. This image does not apply only to the transfer market: Spurs attracts its share of showbiz personalities, 'flash geezers in camel-hair coats', who come to the ground in chauffeur-driven Rolls-Royces, and get stared at by suspicious crowds of skint dole-boys. At big games there are always plenty of ticket touts at White Hart Lane, ready to provide for their expensive customers. It is not only the touts who cash in. At the local derby against Arsenal, fascists in the crowd revive the old Mosleyite chant of 'The yids, the yids, we gotta get rid of the yids.' The casual anti-semitism displayed by some of Spurs rivals, and by some young Spurs themselves, does not mean that the club is a focus for mass anti-semitism. Perceptions are far more confused and split than that. A Chelsea fan I interviewed told me that he hated 'the fucking yids' most of all. I pointed out that I was Jewish. He was unmoved. 'But you're not a Tottenham Hotspur supporter!' (I'm a Chelsea fan, for my sins). Some of the Tottenham fans, meanwhile, decided that 'if you are called Jewish, then be Jewish', and started to turn up at matches wearing skull-caps! Spurs attracts many recruits from Cricklewood, Colindale, Burnt Oak and beyond. The Park Lane End was also among the first London Ends to show a strong black-and-white mix. This cosmopolitanism was dramatically extended to the team itself, with the arrival of two Argentinians, Ardiles and Villa, following their success in the 1978 World Cup. From the Shelf came showers of confetti to welcome their new heroes, just as they do in Buenos Aires. From the Park Lane came chants of 'Ar–gen–ti–na!' Considering their associations with 'unpopular' groups of people such as Jews, blacks and Argentinians, Spurs have been remarkably popular and successful.

**WEST HAM UNITED** Wit is supposed to be the East Enders' secret weapon. You certainly have to have a sense of humour to be a West Ham supporter, and not only because of the team. After the war, West Ham were in the Second Division, and the East End, as elsewhere, was under an austere Labour government. Then came

87

a period of relative affluence in the fifties, but there was still bad housing, boring jobs and, finally, unemployment. But if the East Enders' hopes and dreams of a better life were not fulfilled through the ballot box, there was always the team. And what a team! Hammers have never performed too consistently in the ritual slap-stick of the Saturday League. Two-goal leads were thrown away with regular abandon. The supporters' theme tune was 'We're forever blowing bubbles'. But like most clubs West Ham have had their moments of glory, where the dreams and hopes of their supporters are at least temporarily fulfilled. After twenty-three years in the Second Division, after several typically near-misses, they finally won promotion to the First Division in the sixties. Their new manager, Ron Greenwood (later England manager) was a positive idealist compared with the harsh utilitarianism displayed by most of Britain's soccer bosses. He said: 'Football should reflect the better side of life.' Greenwood's patient nurturing of local talent paid off in 1964 when Hammers won the Cup, incredibly beating Manchester United in the Semi-Final, and almost throwing it away against Second Division Preston in the Final. In 1965 Hammers won the European Cup-Winners' Cup, beating the Germans. 'Boyce is better than Pele, Geoff Hurst is better than Eu—se—bio,' sang the crowd. But this was merely a prelude to greater things: 1966. England – or rather West Ham in the form of the holy trinity of Moore, Peters and Hurst – beat the Germans to win the World Cup. What chance had the German captain 'Kaiser' Franz Beckenbauer and his Meisterfussballers against the doggedness and determination of Bobby Moore and his band of tommies? It was close. It went to extra time. But we muddled through – as usual. In fact 1966 proved something of an Indian summer for English football. It was said that, 'We always play better under Labour.' But by this time Harold Wilson's government was struggling to imitate the Tories. There was a noticeable lack of skill on the political front and the Tories were returned to power. Britain went into Europe and out of the World Cup. West Ham struggled hopelessly to avoid relegation and the club's dock-worker supporters went on strike and still ended up on the dole. In the 'sad, shitty seventies', the politicians' promises of Jerusalem recede: up on the West Ham North Bank, a bovver boy who is busy running with the End calls his unemployed dad 'one of the fucking nothings'.

# Ragazzi di Stadio

Like beat groups, the English soccer Ends have proved to be highly exportable. The popularity of the BBC's 'Match of the Day' is not only confined to Britain; it commands a world-wide audience. Foreign viewers are not only impressed by the hard, competitive quality of English League games but also by their extraordinarily charged atmosphere. Fans from Germany and Holland have even sent over emissaries to observe at first-hand how it is done.

Beppe is leader of The Fighters, an English-style group of 'ragazzi di stadio'[1] who follow Juventus of Turin, one of Italy's greatest clubs, whose core of senior players was largely responsible for Italy winning the 1982 World Cup in Spain. Although he comes from a generally more relaxed and gentle male culture, for Beppe the sheer spectacle of the English Ends is a rich potential source of emulation.

Although Beppe may not himself approve, Italian crowds are often split by politics as much as by football.

'They call me the leader. I don't call myself that. The others call me that, because of the things I have done. I have always stood on the Curve.[2] It was me who organized the group of Juventus fans called The Fighters. So I got known as the leader. I got recognized for the things that I did. You do a lot of things at work you don't get recognition for. In the stadium if you do things you get recognized for it.

'Before The Fighters were formed, we were just a group of kids who were all in the Fossa.[3] Then some of us started to get ideas of our own, and there started to be disagreements. One day we were

1. Stadium boys.
2. The Italian End.
3. Another group of Juventus fans.

all in the Fossa headquarters, and it was clear we had to divide. So we formed The Fighters.

'The idea was a fan club based on the English fans. We would support Juve[4] without using drums and klaxons and this kind of thing. Instead we would do it the English way by holding up our scarves, clapping our hands rhythmically, chanting and so on.'

*'How did you get the name "The Fighters"?'*

'It was invented by a boy who did not even know what the word meant. It just sounded right. Not "fighters" in the sense of hooligans, who go to football to break things up, but "fighters" meaning to organize lots of new things. Of course there are clashes with other fans, with the Commandos of Milan, the Ultras of Torino. Things like this do happen. But this is not the real aim for us.'

*'Have you ever been to a soccer match in England?'*

'Me, personally, no. Some of the others have. I have only seen it on television. And I also have the record of Pink Floyd which has the Liverpool fans singing. In England the stadiums are covered, so that when everybody sings together the sound resounds. I would like it to be like that here. Everybody joining in. I think we are the first in Italy to have an English-style fan club. No drums, just the hand-clapping and scarf-waving. Not that I always want to compare us to the English.'

*'What do you think of the Ultras who follow Torino?'*

'I think good and bad things about them. They are well organized, definitely better than us. But they have money and we haven't. Everything they do is financed by the club. We have to make do with what we can.

'On the other hand I don't respect a lot of the things they do in the stadium. Last year they beat up a woman just because she was wearing a Juve scarf. And it wasn't just that one woman who got beat up. Others have been attacked, including a journalist. Now if they have something against us, let them come to us, try to beat

4. Pronounced 'Yuvé'.

me up even, but they shouldn't beat up people who have nothing to do with it at all. Once I did get beaten up by them. It was after the Juventus *v.* Torino game. Some kids came to me and said, "Let's go and smash up a bus of people who haven't got anything to do with the Ultras!" We got to the car-park before the final whistle, so we had time to smash up their bus and really do a lot of damage. After that we went to the bar in front of the Filadelfia [the Juventus stadium]. But there were a lot more Ultras there, more than there were of us. My friends ran away, and I was left there, and they caught me. Still, I don't hold it against them. One of the boys who beat me up I met a week later at the station. Now you can imagine how it might have turned out! Instead I went up to him and talked to him, and said that we weren't shits and that we could beat him up if we wanted to, but we weren't going to. He said, "I respect you, and I am not just saying that because there are thirty boys behind you." I said, "OK, let's meet up at the next derby game." But he never appeared. Maybe he didn't want to be seen with us there.'

*'Are there splits among The Fighters as well?'*

'Recently some of the kids said they weren't going to come to the stadium any more. They have other ideas. They have become more political. We just couldn't talk with them any more. They were wearing scarves with red tassles, red berets, some of them even wore all red scarves. It was a joke! None of us are all on the left or all on the right. Why make a big thing out of it? Everybody is free to think how they want. Personally, my sympathies are to the left. Not the PCI [Communists] but the Democrazia Proletaria.[5] But I know people, right-wing people, who I can talk to. A lot of them were once on the left, too.

'For me, being a Juve fan comes first, before anything else. I started supporting them when I was a child and I have continued ever since. All my friends are there. I can talk with any of them there. I don't make any distinctions. If somebody is on the left, or on the right, it doesn't matter. You can even talk about politics, argue your ideas

5. A small party to the left of the PCI.

with them, and it won't end in fights like in other places. Because when the team comes out on to the field, then who gives a shit? We are all behind the Juve! We all shout for them, we try to help the team to win. And we help each other, too. Quite a few times some of us have been stuck outside the ground because we haven't got enough money to buy a ticket. All you have to do is tell everybody else, and then we have a whip-round. Everyone puts in a hundred lire, until there is enough to buy a ticket and maybe get a sandwich at half-time. This is great, in my opinion. Our only interest should be to support Juve.'

*'What do you think of the Juventus players?'*

'We Fighters have got fed-up with the Juve players. We have had enough. All the match there are only two players who come over and say "hello" and give a wave to the people on the Curve – Bennetti and Tardelli. The others are very distant. What we wanted most was that the Juve players did a lap of honour around the field, and then would stop by the Curve and talk with us for at least half an hour. Instead they do the lap of honour around the field and then they rush off to the changing-rooms, and we are left completely disillusioned. They cheat us.

'This is sad. For me the players represent all that is beautiful, even if they are big-headed. They think they are supermen just because they play for the Juve. They are not really interested in anything. The day that Bettega leaves us – so? He goes. We support them. It's they who don't support us. I don't expect Juve to win every match. They could even lose more. But I would like to see them making more of an effort in every match – to give something back to the fans, to the people who always support them.'

*'During a match you sometimes chant "The public is shit" ...'*

'That is because most of the people who come to watch Juve really are shit! Maybe the fault is with the players who are so cold and don't wind up the public as they should. But if you took away The Fighters, The Fossi and Superstar [a smaller fan group], the rest of them on the Curve are not real fans of the Juve. They don't applaud. They don't get excited. Not even when there's a beautiful move. They whistle if somebody makes a bad pass. That's not being real fans. I read an article by Kevin Keegan, who used to play for Liverpool. He wrote that "... in England the most important thing in football is not the players, not the clubs, but the *fans*".'

# Rolled-up White Jeans and Doc Martens

What were the girls doing while the boys were putting the boot in on the terraces? Many were up there with them. According to most kids I talked to, girl fans fell into three distinct categories: 'There's the quiet ones. They just go to watch the match. Then there's the girlfriends of the boys. They will just go with their bloke. Then there's the scrubbers. They go down in twos and threes, sometimes more. They stand up the back of the End. They don't go to watch the match. Boys come up to 'em, try to put their arms around 'em. When they try to touch 'em up, they start crying out. They are harder than the boys, some of them girls are. They wear rolled-up white jeans and Doctor Martens [boots]. They get stuck into you if you get on the wrong side of 'em.'

The more sexist elements among the boys readily proclaimed their opposition to extending terrace rights and privileges to those they considered second-class citizens, both in this male preserve and elsewhere. Reasons ranged from the blatantly chauvinistic – 'I hate seeing girls at a match. I would rather go to a match alone than with a bird' – to appeals to dubious codes of male chivalry and protectiveness – 'I wouldn't take girlfriend. Kids would be trying to feel their arse all t'time. They can get raped in Kop. When Liverpool score everybody dives on 'em. You can't stop it. The ones that do go must enjoy it.'

Among little Enders – the children – girls add a familiar air of playground horseplay: 'There was these two Coventry fans on the train. All the kids jump on 'em, trying to get their trousers down. Then two other girls jump out and start laying in to the boys. Then this kid kicked one of the Coventry girls. And this other kid smashed him in the face – for hitting a girl, like ...'

Where older girls' gangs do exist there is nothing 'put on' about them. Some set out not only to emulate but to outdo the boys by exploiting sexual as well as End rivalries. These 'Leeds Angels' describe how they, and the tougher girls who follow Man. United, Norwich and Ipswich especially, have carved their names with pride in the mythologies of terrace aggro: 'We go to fight. We come from Seacroft. At Newcastle we were getting chucked out of ground. We had no scarves on. We were pointing boys we knew out to coppers, just for a laugh. They were getting their heads kicked in and we were laughing. Then we joined in the fighting. At Norwich and Ipswich, there's sometimes more lasses support them than boys. They say [to the boys] "I'll meet you at the station afterwards." Then they mug 'em! When Man. United played Norwich, and the Stretford burned down their stand, there were forty arrests and must have been thirty lasses got arrested.'

For the mainstream of working-class girls, however, football and all its rough associations are very much off-limits; especially among those who put stress on a good appearance, cleanliness, good manners, etc., and aspire to traditionally high feminine-status jobs such as secretaries and hairdressers. For some, being decked out in scarves and rosettes by a disappointed dad who wanted a son could leave them with a lifelong detestation of football and other male-dominated pastimes. Also, going out with an 18-year-old whose first loves are football and fighting can be a frustrating experience, and is usually interpreted as a sign of his immaturity and even weakness. 'But if you really want him, you have to *wait* until he grows out of it' – until, that is, he falls in love, which pulls him out from his mates faster than any copper, and is ready for the responsibilities of marriage and a family.

Yet, like rock music, football can accommodate the very different adolescent experiences of boys and girls. Thousands of girls – 'the quiet ones' – are committed fans in their own right, every bit as passionate and knowledgeable as any boy.

Joanna Burns, aged sixteen, is an Aston Villa supporter like her father and grandfather – in this case a cause for parental concern!

'I'm a tomboy, really, cos I'm not like a girl. My bedroom is painted claret and blue colours, with a big picture of the Villa team. It's been signed by some of the players. I wanted it to be in claret and blue *stripes*, but my dad won't allow that. So I had to have a patterned paper of claret and blue. My mum and dad think I'm, you know, too much of a boy. My mum doesn't like us – my sister and me – to go down the match cos of the swearing. My mum and dad are conservative compared to some families. If I just wanted claret and blue on the walls and it was nothing to do with football, I don't think she would have minded. I was gonna put scarves up and everything, but she said no. So I did the best I could which is one picture of the team.

'Some girls, they *just* go for the players. But I go down and watch the football as well. When you go to the Villa, at the ground entrance, as you walk in to pay your money, it's got BOYS, OAPS, and MEN over the turnstiles. Sometimes the boys say things like, "Oh, it's a girl!" and things like that. But very rarely. Only when they are drunk, like Glasgow Rangers fans when they came, being a girl is really terrible then.

'Up the End, there's more boys than men, but there are quite a few girls as well. More and more girls go, although a lot of their mothers don't like it. Some girls go in packs. They are out for trouble. They even join in the fighting with the boys, or encourage 'em. But you get that in school – girls fighting – even when there's no boys around.

'When I first started going to football, I used to think, "Oh, if only I could be a boy and be out there, in the limelight, being a footballer." A lot of girls don't dream of being players, they just dream of being with the players, meeting the players. It's usually the boys that want the stardom, to be just like the players, while the girls would be content with just meeting the person that they have worshipped for so long. Cos it is like worshipping them, really.

'When you watch the players, you can't but notice the good-looking ones. You see them on TV, how they speak, what their personalities are like.'

*'Are they like pop stars?'*

'Yes, they are. It is like seeing a pop group in a concert sometimes. You have that atmosphere. Like going to a pop concert every week! Really good! I have pop idols. I used to be really mad on David Essex. It varies. He's out of reach a lot more than the football players are, because seeing them on the pitch, you are near them. Although there's thousands of people in the same position as you that want to get near them. They are *there* in Birmingham. David Essex is completely out of reach. I went to his concert. It was fabulous. But afterwards you think, Well, I won't see him until his next concert, or on TV, and TV isn't as good. There's no atmosphere.

'You're interested in the older players, how they play, their form. But the younger players are nearer to you. Robson, he's not old, but further afield from my age than, say, John Deehan. You have your own ideas who the good-looking players are. When the *Villa Times* was out, they publicized that John Deehan was engaged. The girls at school sat down and gazed at the photograph and said, "He's engaged!" As if to say, "I've got no chance now!" I've never met any of the Villa players. But you can always dream, and imagine what they are like. If you can't meet them you have to imagine them.

'Everyone dreams of things and thinks of things. When you are sitting on a bus you think about the football and you can imagine ... I dream, I dream about meeting the players and talking to them. But I know that if I knew them all and if I was like *that* with them I'd find some other – there will always be something that you can't reach, that you can go after and look up to, which you can never reach, which is the Aston Villa players for me. Cos I mean, I will never know them, most likely won't even talk to any of them, but it's something that you can imagine and dream about.

'When the Holte End is at its best your nerves are all on edge. You feel as if you are not the only one. You feel right with the club then, one big happy family. If you lose you could sit down and cry cos you get that tense. Sometimes you just wanna run on the pitch and go mad. When I went to Sunderland, when we went up to the First Division, we ran on the pitch at the end and it was all happy.

'You let go. You can be yourself. No one says anything against you. If you go out with friends, you are always conscious of what they think, or if you are doing things right. But up the Holte End, everyone's the same, you've all got scarves, you all support the club. You have got one thing in common, everyone has. Where, if you go out with friends, you can have different ideas and arguments can start.

'You're there, you're watching the football, and afterwards you're

97

not with anyone then, are you? Some people don't care so much. They just go to a game on a Saturday and that's it. For me it goes deeper. I could be interested in another club, but for me the Villa is *it*.

'You go to enjoy yourself. Everyone has to get away and enjoy themselves. But you can also understand things better. You can learn about different people at a football match. About different attitudes. You find out who are the people you don't like, who think things and say things that you don't like, which you wouldn't learn if you just sat at home and watched it on "Match of the Day". You see, some people come to the game in Jaguars, and they are all dressed-up, no scarves or anything. They sit there, you can see them sitting there in the expensive seats. There's no excitement there. They might be shareholders, directors. They just sit there like statues and watch.'

# Schoolboy Saturday

'As soon as our children are able to walk,
they are labelled as hooligans. Now why is that?'

Polish shipyard worker

In Barrie Keeffe's play *Gotcha* (1977)[1] a muscle-bound P E instructor
is about to indulge in some lunchtime intimacy with a woman teacher
in the privacy of the school Science stockroom. A spotty youth
interrupts them. He has come to collect his motorbike and is struck
and insulted for his pains. But this is his last day at school and
he cracks up – 'There's a pain in me head!' He holds a lighted match
near the tank of his motorbike. Gotcha! At the pupil's request, the
Head is summoned, and the enraged boy assails his former mentors
with all the pent-up frustration of five years at the receiving end
of an education system that promised him everything and gave him
nothing. For, like Shirley Williams's Great Debate of the seventies,
where all the crucial decisions had already been taken, the boy's
background had decided his fate in advance. At one point the boy
forces the Head to agree that he could become a brain surgeon if
he wanted – 'if you apply yourself, work hard'. However, none of
the hostages can remember the future brain surgeon's name. To them
he's just one of the 'choc ice and vinegar crisps lunch club' of school
failures. You know, a bit of a nutter, a loner, no gang pull: 'There's
one in every class' as the teachers would say.

Thousands of pupils and teachers would recognize themselves in
*Gotcha*: on the one side, 'puny, spotty, skinny yobbo, with a
chromium-plated leer'; on the other, 'decency, endeavour, order'.

Class inequality has long been the acne on the face of British
education: 'We used to have kids come to our school. They were
dressed the best. We came from the council estate. They came from
a sort of middle-class housing estate. Those kids, you can bet your
life, those kids were treated well. They got the most attention. The
teachers turned their attention to them. They stood out. They could

1. Part of Barrie Keeffe's trilogy *Gimme Shelter*, Eyre Methuen, 1979.

go home and sit in a decent house and do homework. We had kids running about the house and all stuck in three rooms. What chance have we got to compete with that? The only chance we've got is to stick together.'

In the spring of 1971, in London, Birmingham, Manchester and other big cities, state secondary schools were hit by a wave of mass pupil strikes and protests. The Schools Action Campaign was led in the main by dissident sixth-formers in rehearsal for becoming student militants. But as this was the time of the miners' strike against the Tory government, and worker militancy was in the air, the Campaign found a strong response among working-class pupils in the lower streams. 'There was a couple of hippies – I dunno what they were – hippies or somink – and they was giving out leaflets about the school strike outside the gates, and they was telling us our rights. Saying: What's your rights? Why should you get caned? Why should you get detention for something you didn't do? Why should you wear uniforms? Why should you do the work they set you? Why not work by yourselves and set your own work? We was all gonna go for it. Someone burned down the prefects' room. The headmistress calls up a big meeting in the hall. She was having goes at us. And all the people at the back, they was having goes back. A lot of 'em just walked out of the school.'

For a moment the authorities seemed paralysed. Gotcha? 'Then they was writing home, sending letters to parents, making threats.'

For revolutionaries, 1971 may have been the Year of the School-kid: the strikes were greeted with a hysterical press response – 'The barbarians are at the gates!' – but they received virtually no support from adult workers' organizations. Moreover, the splits between the nascent National Union of School Students and the more militant Schools Action Union contained all the familiar seeds of left divisiveness. Pupil Power still seemed to mean power for the future students. But what of the rest? 'It's very difficult, when you're living on an estate, and you're going to school, and you know what's going to happen to you. How can you relate to a debate which says "The Marxist position is ..."'? What's that got to do with my wanting to be a hairdresser? What's it got to do with anything? That's why I left S A U. Some people joined the Y C L, some joined S L L [Socialist Labour League] and some went into the Labour Party. And they are still having little factional arguments. And you would say, "What the hell has this got to do with the kids at school?" It all sounded great till I went back to school on Monday.' From another pupil came a similarly pessimistic response: 'It weren't worth it, cos it would never come off, a strike, trying to get it by yourself, just all the children in the school. You gotta have a teacher, some teachers behind yer . . .'

As the strikes fizzled out, Valderma balm was quickly proffered in the form of toothless Schools Councils, a more liberalized curriculum, more concerned, sympathetic head teachers. And the mass of pupils settled down to serving what many still saw as custodial sentences, albeit in open prisons. For the gut impatience with school when you could be out in the world earning a wage had always been the dismay of the most liberal educational reformers.

Although it was always unlikely that '277,000 youngsters will find themselves by staying on at school', the raising of the school-leaving age in 1972 has served to increase the educational system's custodial policing function, as the demand for youth labour has decreased. Meanwhile, left to itself, playground politics took a rapid swing to the right. In 1978 the National Front officially announced its schools campaign, focusing on the slogan 'Get the Red teachers'.

As a schoolkid you may be powerless, but there are other places where you can assert control, or at least *feel* that you are doing so. In the mid-seventies the population of the soccer Ends had got noticeably younger, as older members departed or were removed. End life became less gang-hierarchical in character, more like a chaotic school playground, with burly policemen instead of teachers to keep you in line.

Alfie, aged thirteen, and Colin, his mate, lived opposite Arsenal's ground.

COLIN: We do kick each other, pissing around in the playground. In class it's just a messabout, innit?

ALFIE: At football you go down the front where all your mates go.

COLIN: I've been chucked into the cage at Arsenal. When Jeff Blockley come down, everyone was singing, 'Blockley is a wanker,' and we was just singing it and a copper got hold of us and goes, 'You'll do.' So we says, 'What about the rest of 'em up the back?'

101

He goes, 'I'm coming back for them later.' We got chucked in this pen, about two hundred kids in there, squashed up like sardines. And about half an hour later they chucked us out of the ground. But we got back in. The gates opened five minutes before the end. We crept back in.

ALFIE: One time my mate steps back and on one of a copper's toes by accident. The copper grabbed his arm and pushed him on to the crash-barriers.

COLIN: If you spit on the floor you get your arm nearly broken. They nick you for anything.

ALFIE: When it's cold we start a little fire and sing:

> We're all nice and warm
> We're all nice and warm
> It's nice and dry
> It's nice and dry in 'ere.

COLIN: We got lots of songs. When it rains we sing:

> We get cold
> We get wet
> WE HAVEN'T BEEN TAKEN YET!

If the school had failed to provide accessible role models for kids like this, there were plenty of legends and reputations being passed down and around the little Ends. Older hands began to refer to this process as 'just a bunch of kids, acting like they're older, thinking they are hard'. Fourteen-year-old 'little hard nuts' like Ian Murray, from Birmingham, constantly in trouble at school, crop-headed and face badly scarred by a Stanley knife, said: 'When there's no away fans, we just fight among ourselves. The other week, a crap match, the left side of the Holte [Aston Villa] and the right side of the Holte were fighting. I got arrested for flicking lighted fag ends down the End. The copper grabs me and I went to court next day and got fined thirty quid. We had a whip round up the Holte to pay it off. They take me for like leader.'

Not all schoolchildren leave all moral sense behind as soon as they enter the ground. For Chris Hughes, aged fifteen, the game itself is the centre of attention; it means excitement, instead of the boredom of school life: 'I got my report last year. It said in it "concentrates more on football than he does on maths".'

'Sitting in a class for forty minutes, and hearing the teacher shouting at yer, and hearing the chalk on the board, BAM! – fifteen over four, fifteen times four – you get bored with it and you got nothing to say about it. So you say to your next-door neighbour, "Arsenal played well Saturday, they should 'ave won." The teacher catches you and sends you out. It's boring just sitting there, just looking at figures on a board, just copying 'em down. Half the time they don't describe it to yer, know what I mean? They just put it up on the board and say, "Copy it!", and you copy it without knowing what you are doing. When you put your hand up, they say they are busy marking, so you can't win ... I got a little job of an evening. I put money away. I get a fiver. So I put £2.50 away, spend the other £2.50 on anything I feel that I want. But if I want more money I just put an extra 50p away and it covers it – the away travel. £4.50 to get to Bristol City this season, so I could afford that. The supporters club is supposed to be cheaper but it isn't. £4.15 to go to Bolton!'

*'Do your parents mind you spending money on football?'*

'My mum does. She don't like football a lot. But me dad, he don't mind as long as I don't get in trouble. He used to support them [Arsenal], but he calls them a load of wallies now. He says, "They couldn't kick their way out of a paper bag." He says, "You never know, you could come 'ome one day with thirty stitches up there, you could be knifed or something. It's not nice!" He says, "Keep out of trouble!" We don't look for trouble. We just stand there, watch the game, and half-time, do all the competitions in the programme.

'I go in the North Bank. With five mates. We all meet each other outside the pub near the Arsenal, the George Robey. We arrange it. Every week when we're at home, you got the feeling that we'll win, you know. You got the feeling that your team's gonna win. On Saturday you'd 'ave thought that we'd beat Coventry 3–nil. In the end they turned out nearly to beat us 3–nil. So you can't win 'em all like. And you can't lose 'em all. That's the way I look at it.

'It's a better feeling when they do win. It makes you feel sort of happy. Like you could go over there in a sort of grumpy mood.

Minute by minute it's cheering you up, and by the end of the game you go out with your heart content, full of football. You can't describe it to anyone then. If you had a boring game, and you have lost 3–nil at home, then you just walk away. When Ipswich come down and beat us 4–1, I just walked home at half-time. That was it. I thought, No way we could come back. So me and my mates just went. We took our scarves off.

'We don't look for trouble. We went down to the bar one time when Man. United come down. They look at yer [the United fans]. One of 'em went up to one of our kids and bought 'im a drink and went back to where he come from. He just bought him a drink and went back. So the kid says "thanks" like and walked off the other way. When the game starts they forget, and then they start singing, and it all erupts.

'You do get carried away sometimes. You got all the rest shouting and swearing behind you, so it carries you away. Me and my mates started swearing one time. The policeman, he told us to shut it, so we just shut it like, else we get chucked out. But he was keeping an eye on us, just looking back over his shoulder all the time.

'The coppers, they are all right, but they are a bit hard. They get 'em, the kids, especially if they are only little – and I'm not all that small really! They get littler kids than me and they twist their arms and they pull their hair so they can't see cos their heads are in the air and they trip 'em up at the same time, and run 'em into the van. My older brother, he just reckons they are Nazis, that's what he calls 'em. He just shouts out "Nazis" to the police. He don't like them. He don't like the National Front either. Nor do I.'

*'Why not?'*

'It's just like football violence starting all over again, innit? Two rival supporters again. Say you was coloured, and I'm sitting 'ere white, and you was to call me a name. Straightaway my instinct would be to get up and hit you or somink, wouldn't it? So it revolves all around in one circle. That's the way I look at it.'

*'Why do you think that racist chants are starting to be heard from the terraces?'*

'I dunno. I can't understand it. My family have lived in Holloway for a long time. They are just the same as white people, ain't they? Built the same, everyone's the same. It's all right some of 'em up the North Bank shouting out "National Front", but what they don't remember is that there's coloured in the football grounds themselves. You got 'em at Arsenal, Spurs, you get 'em everywhere. They are mixed in with white people and in groups. They don't do no harm to anybody. I'm not prejudiced or racialist, neither is my family.

'It makes me sick sometimes. They shouldn't taunt the players cos they are coloured. It's not just the coloureds. I went to Coventry a couple of years ago, with some of me mates. At Arsenal there's mostly Irish footballers – I have got nothing against them either! – and they got out on the field and as soon as Liam Brady got the ball it was "Kill the Irish! Kill the Irish!" from the Coventry supporters. [This was the time of the I R A Birmingham pub bombing.] Brady had half an hour of that and he walked off. The substitute come on. Hearing all them chants he just walked off.'

*'What do you like best about Arsenal?'*

'Watching Alan Hudson play. He's got real good skill. Good control. He'll lose it or the ball will roll away from him, but he will never slide tackle the bloke to get the ball. They try and jockey him, or hustle him off it. He just stands there and hopes that the geezer miskicks it. That's good. That's what I like. He's a lazy bugger, though. Two weeks out of the side with a sprained fingernail . . .'

One night I dreamt that one
day I was in the crowd
watching England *v.* France.
It was such a boring game
that nearly everyone was
leaving. When a player
came off, Sir Alf Ramsey
was just going to send some
one on when I jumped over
the fence, ran to where he
was sitting and begged him
if I could play. The ref
went and consulted Alf, but
he said I could play. The

game went on and I done a
solo run up to the goal
line. I didn't want to
become too selfish so I
passed it to Geoff Hurst,
and with no one in the goal,
not even the goalie, he
walked it up to the line,
ran back a little way, shot,
and it went wide. I stood
there wondering why Alf puts
stupid West Ham players like
him in the team. With five
minutes to go and the score
0–0, I collected a pass just
outside the area. I turned
quickly and shot. It hit
the bar, then hit the post,
then it went in. Everybody
cheered. At the end of the
match I received my first
England cap.

Peter Goodman, aged fifteen

# Return of the Hard Men

'Moral insanity, criminality, uncontrolled animality – call it what you will. Psychiatrists called it "psychopathic personality" or, same thing, "sociopathic personality". It meant you were antisocial. In terms of accountability before the law, it was equal to sanity.'

Norman Mailer, *The Executioner's Song*

Worried Chelsea supporter (1977): 'These days it's getting *really* bad. The violence. They don't seem to care what they do to people. As long as they don't get caught, they don't mind. They ain't got no conscience at all. They just do it for the enjoyment. [They are] the leaders, mainly: Mad Mick of the Chelsea Shed, Wolfman. Big fellas. They ain't kids . . .'

By the late seventies, scenes such as the following were common on soccer terraces all over the country: 'There's a bunch of kids, couldn't have been older than fourteen, fifteen. A big muscly bloke comes over. 'E must 'ave been about thirty. 'E says, " 'Ere, you lot, I'm gonna kill you." All the kids said, "Ah no, forget it, we got nowt against you!" And they just walked away. Scared! Then 'e went up to some other kids and said, "I'm Millwall." Then 'e piled into 'em. No warning, nothing.'

At Wolves, some young fans told me how a squad of full-grown adult men, some with beards, and wearing heavy overcoats, had come to take over the terrace action from the teenagers: 'They ain't kids no more, the leaders now. They're blokes, about twenty-eight, thirty years of age, and big blokes an' all. They're always marching at the front now, when you're marching out of away grounds, looking for the bovver, especially if you've lost. They don't walk to ground. They come in cars. They're huge. The kids know 'em – but only to look at, like. You don't argue with 'em. They lead. And that's how all the *serious* bovver starts. There's one down there – he's huge – about twenty stones. They call 'im "Hippo". And there's Eggy, his mate, with his nose all flattened. They're heroes to the little kids.'

But men like Eggy and Hippo were usually quick to make it clear that the soccer terrace was just one of a number of stamping-grounds. Hippo explained: 'Us lot, the blokes who really go to fight, we don't just fight inside the football ground. We fight outside the ground.

107

We go to discos and fight. We go to nightclubs and have a fight. In a pub we have a fight. Wherever we go we fight ... No, we don't do it for money. Hell's Angels, mercenary groups, the villains round 'ere, they will do it for the money. But you've got others, they just go around and they just wanna do it for the *feeling* of smashing someone's head open. I mean – sometimes I just feel I wanna get hold of some cunt and lay him over a railing and splatter him. Other times you may feel sorry after. But not often. [*Laughs.*] Mostly you just wanna hit someone every time.'

Many of the End leaders of the late seventies, like Hippo, had been prominent graduates of the terrace class of 1968. They made their reputations in those chaotic early days. But once 'born on the North Bank' they gradually passed on into an early marriage, a not-so-steady job, having kids, on and off the dole, a spell 'inside', perhaps. Ten years of the pain and stress of adult life takes its toll – marital breaks-ups, more brushes with the Law. One solution is to go back with the boys again, where once you held sway. For the ageing hard nut, being outnumbered fifty to one in a back alley by rival fans is a fond memory compared with holding down a menial job without prospects, and coming home to an angry wife who is demanding to know what has happened to the housekeeping money.

One such casualty of domestic strife is Leggo, who left school at thirteen, like most of his close mates, and started following Millwall FC as a teenager in the late sixties. In 1978, men like Leggo and his friends became an overnight cause of national concern following a BBC television documentary on crowd violence at Millwall. This small South London neighbourhood team had begun to develop a reputation for violence among its supporters that it had seldom enjoyed as a result of its achievements on the field. (Previously, the dilapidated Cold Blow Lane ground had been affectionately referred to in soccer circles as home of 'the best team in the Old Kent Road'.) Now three mobs of its supporters were causing concern, and successfully deterring both away-team visitors and respectable locals from paying a visit to the ground. The first was a group of young men in their late twenties and early thirties, known as F-troop. A 'bunch of nutters who got involved in ruckin' every chance', they favoured wearing surgical masks and butchers' coats spattered with blood. They were the leaders. The next group, the Halfway Line, were teenage hard-core supporters who followed home and away games and were prepared to 'steam in on the aggro' when necessary. Finally there was the youngest group, who were a children's version of the Halfway Line. A whole career was possible through support on the terraces, from the age of ten to about thirty years old, and people like Leggo, aged twenty-seven and upwards, were in the top class: 'There's me in the thick of the ruckin'. What you gonna be called? A coward? Look at 'im over there, not steamin' in, is that what I want 'em to say? ... I 'ave been married. We're separated now. She always said, "Just so as you got enough money to go see Millwall, that does you." I'm workin' at the moment. When I'm out of work I just do odd jobs 'ere and there. I respect any bloke who don't run and can stand there and have a good fight. Me, personally, I won't take verbal when we go away. I won't take it from a northerner. I followed this club *years*, and I mean *years*, and I'm not going away with the team for some dirty northern ponce to spit all over me. If he spits all over me, I'll cut his head with a wine-glass ... You do it for the reputation of the club. We're not thugs. We got standards. Not like Man. United or Chelsea. If there was a woman with a baby, and we was havin' a ruck, they'd all help that woman out of the way and then carry on with the ruckin' ... I been inside a few times. Last one was for brickin' this Paki. I'm not 100 per cent for the NF. But you help out, like. You gotta think, "We're all here, everyone works, got 'omes here." Then you see these Asian families just come off the banana boat. On the Lewisham march[1] there was a hundred of the Millwall against the Reds ... You'll never change Millwall. Twenty-five thousand all-seat stadium, this sort of thing. They want families to come. But you'll never change it. It's your mates down there, mates you rely on, they go everywhere with you, you go around the country with 'em ...'

The return of the hard men meant that terrace aggro was robbed of its playful quality of ritualized wargame. The hard men meant business and a whole new generation of fans had emerged who had to be prepared to accept previously undreamt-of extremes of violence. The new End heroes' fantasies belonged less in the world

---

1. A large anti-National-Front demonstration organized by the Anti-Nazi League in 1977.

of 'teenage rampage', more in the psychological wasteland of the sadist and the solitary killer. Was the Yorkshire Ripper a hero to the people who one Saturday afternoon on the Leeds Kop goaded the police with chants of, 'You'll never catch the Ripper' and '11–0' (referring to the number of the Ripper's victims)? If you are hounded and branded as animals, perhaps the reasoning goes, then you might as well *be* animals. The moment when people decide to reject absolutely basic rules of decent behaviour invariably corresponds with society's absolute rejection of them. There are those who do not simply intend to watch the moral order fall apart. They want to speed up the process, to reinforce the mood of pessimism and despair that society feels about ever finding a cure for 'mindless hooliganism'.

For the vast majority of those who get involved in aggro, however, even the most nihilistic acts are usually no more than an overture to conformism: kicking a copper in the head before caving in to the inescapable pressures of finding and holding down a job, getting married, raising a family. 'You don't believe in any of it, but you do it anyway.' The hard-man, though, lives in a more dangerous and unchanging world. Permanently sensitized to 'trouble' in his environment, his paranoid fantasies about defending his 'patch' against outsiders make him ripe for manipulation by the politics of the extreme right. At Millwall, during the 1977 season, out of a home gate of 3,500, some two hundred young men were sighted standing shoulder to shoulder in para-military uniform, displaying the insignia of the National Front and of the British Movement.

# Colour of Your Scarf, Colour of Your Skin

There was a time when the soccer terrace was a place where black and white youth could find common ground, even in towns where for the rest of the week they might be making rival claims to being 'top mob' on the streets. In Wolverhampton, for example: 'Any other day of the week it's gang warfare between blacks and whites. Except on a Saturday afternoon. You're the best of mates because you've got the same scarf on. It's like being in the army. It's like the Germans fighting the English. If you see someone in a red and white scarf fighting someone in a blue and white scarf, you just go and join with 'em and that's it. You're with 'em for the rest of the afternoon... You've got less chance of being beaten up if you're a black kid than if you had a Blues [Birmingham City] scarf down the Villa.'

Traditionally, team support has provided a useful way for migrants to the big cities, such as the Irish, to join in popular expressions of local pride and partisanship. Children from a West Indian immigrant background have proved no exception. Indeed, black youth's overwhelming identification with football was established in preference to an allegiance to cricket, the game of the West Indian parent generation. Growing up working-class in England means that a place in the school or club soccer team is a more realistic path to success and recognition. The new black contribution to football was welcomed by progressive coaches and team managers – here was a potential source of much-needed skill and flair which might eventually transform the increasingly sterile English professional game. But in the middle seventies, against a background of an escalating level of terrace violence, tougher methods of crowd control, and rising costs of ground admission and travel, the appearance of black players in the top teams also provoked a more negative response: 'We went to West Brom this Saturday with the Blues, and they was all singing, "National Front." There was this coloured player, Regis [for West

Brom]. They was all singing, "Regis, Regis, gimme that banana."
Then they were singing, "Nigger, nigger, lick my boots," "Tarzan
want a monkey," and stuff like this. After that they started to run
round town after the match singing, "We hate wogs." The Blues have
got a song about Wolves: "The Molyneux is colourful, the Molyneux
is colourful. Full of blacks, full of coons, full of niggers, the Molyneux
is colour–ful." It's cos of all the blackies in the Wolves crowd. Loads
of blackies. Blackies everywhere. You can spot 'em a mile off. All
the blackies walking down the street.'

For this fan, coming from a largely immigrant neighbourhood
of Birmingham (Handsworth), it was quite easy to feel threatened
by (as well as envious) of what he saw as the superior cohesive strength
shown by black youth. White youngsters often *feel* outnumbered,
even though statistically they are not (this is one reason why ten
years of the immigration numbers game played by right-wing politicians such as Enoch Powell has had such a pernicious effect). And
now blacks, through players like Cyril Regis and Laurie Cunningham, were making their presence felt on the field of play itself.

This is not to say that a lot of split perception did not operate.
Regis and Cunningham, for example, were heroes to West Bromwich
fans, black *and* white. And many fans were at pains to insist to me
that racist chants were 'just to get at the other away fans and *their*
black players. If we had one he would be all right. And they shout
out "National Front" cos they know the N F hates wogs, don't they?
Most of 'em don't understand though. They think the N F is *just*
about hating wogs. They chant "National Front", but they haven't
a clue what it's about.' However, during the 1977–8 season, a time
when the fortunes of the National Front were running relatively high,
the Anti-Nazi League decided to intervene directly on the terraces.
The A N L's 'Soccer Fans against the Nazis' campaign enlisted the
support of 'enlightened' soccer managers such as Brian Clough and
Jack Charlton. This added a further injection of divisive politics and,
although the A N L soccer campaign may not have made any con-
verts, it probably helped those decent-minded fans who were
offended by what was going on to stand up and be counted: 'The
Anti-Nazi League leaflets, they're good. I hate National Front cos
of what it's doing, what it's causing. How do coloured people feel
when they've got to sit down and hear about repatriation and all

this? Maggie Thatcher, she's just as bad, she wants to stop immigration, don't she? She's round the twist, makes me sick, 'er . . .'

At the other extreme, some lads were already being recruited from the Ends to take part in the highly publicized NF marches and demonstrations. However, such a step was often less about political commitment, more about the chances of a good scrap – and it didn't really matter who the targets were. In 1977, for example, some Leeds Koppites travelled to Levenshulme, Manchester, where an NF 'protest' march was due to take place: 'But they only went for t'fighting. They only went to Levenshulme to fight. Yeah, they went to fight for NF, but police were there to protect 'em, so when there was no fighting they got bored and they started fighting against 'em [the NF marchers]. It's easier to grab the bloke beside you, innit? So cos they were with 'em they started fighting against National Front then! It was just for fighting, nowt else.'

This incident, however laughable, proved to be among the first signs of more serious attempts at racist coordination of young soccer fans. It also revealed just how much confusion existed among the young about politics, left *and* right. As one fan put it: 'We don't know enough about politics, kids our age, leaving school, and all we know about politics is what we read in the papers or what our parents tell us: Anti-Nazi League, fascists, Nazis, Chilean generals, South Africa – all their slogans, written on walls. And they give you leaflets, try and sell you papers. Why waste your money on it? Socialists, they come up to you in town, on the street. Socialist Worker, they say they are. I think they're communists, aren't they? The *Star* newspaper, that's communist, innit? Me dad don't like 'em, so I s'pose I won't either.'

Alarmed at the level of sheer ignorance about basic political concepts, and the growing tendency to extremism, the liberal political establishment launched a campaign for compulsory political education in schools. Politicians from all the major parties united in the call for 'a modest requirement of school timetable hours in politics'. But who would do the educating? How could 'balance' and 'fairness' be guaranteed? Besides, if the messages of the major parties were preached by teachers, youth-workers and 'straight' political spokesmen – the voices of middle-class authority – would they not be rejected by working-class youth as just one more boring imposition on their school time? While the debate about political education raged, however, the ultra-right were already preparing to step into the breach.

In the 1979 General Election, the National Front, despite some success in making racism respectable to the electorate, made a disastrous showing at the polls. Significantly, this was followed by a far more organized and concerted racist campaign on the terraces. According to a report of the Centre for Contemporary Studies,[1] a group that monitors the activities of the ultra-right, in 1980 the campaign in the football grounds became a priority tactic in fascist recruitment efforts. The National Front's youth paper *Bulldog*, for example, devoted a regular column to its articles 'On the Football Front'. Appealing for membership, *Bulldog* called upon young soccer fans to 'join the fight for your race and nation'. Addressing himself to 'the inner-city kids' one contributor wrote that 'To us whites football is a one-day-in-the-week outlet; on the other six days, white youth have to endure a race-mixing nightmare ... outnumbered and continually harassed by Mafia-type gangs of blacks ... often with the backing of left-wing teachers.' This recruitment campaign was supplemented by the sale of all kinds of paraphernalia: lapel badges, scarves and T-shirts bearing the logo of the National Front or of the British Movement entwined with that of the football club. In London one result of this campaign was that the few black boys who remained in the Ends were either beaten up and driven out, or were tolerated as pet mascots – 'He's *the black* of Upton Park!' – joining in or even in some bizarre cases, as at Arsenal, *leading* the chorus of racial obscenities.

The chants of '*sieg heil*' are also often accompanied by a rampant and recognizable anti-semitism. Arsenal fans wear badges proclaiming 'I hate Tottenham yids'[2] and a record by The Sex Bristols, was reportedly on sale around the ground, containing the verse: 'He's only a poor little yiddo. His face is all battered and torn. He makes me sick so I hit him with a brick, and now he doesn't sing anymore.'

The new End diet of unrestrained racist propaganda is also inter-

1. 'Football and the Fascists', CCS, January 1981.
2. Tottenham Hotspur are commonly referred to as 'the yids', because of their large Jewish following.

spersed with obscene chants and gestures directed against gay people and women.

According to the CCS report, 'Football and the Fascists', there is no question that these recent developments have been in any way spontaneous, as have other phases through which the soccer scene has passed. The British Movement and the National Front, they point out, openly sell their publications outside the grounds, principally at Chelsea, West Ham and Arsenal. On the terraces the activists form into small cells and attach themselves to what the CCS describes as 'the thug elements' in the crowds. Estimates vary as to the numbers involved in these cells. A Chelsea official told the CCS that the number does not exceed a hundred. But a club spokesman also told the *Daily Star*: 'People who in fact are NF mingle with the crowd and make out they are supporters ... At a recent match with Cambridge United there were about 1,500 National Front supporters round the town wearing Chelsea scarves. Some of the lads handing out NF leaflets are about sixteen. They don't know a thing about politics.'

This was an orchestrated political campaign, then, trading on frustration and political confusion. But this disquieting fact remains as well: it is in Britain alone that overt Nazi groups have managed to win a sympathetic response from a significant section of proletarian youth who all other parties have given up as too stupid or apathetic for attention.[3]

3. In Italy, where strong political milieux of both socialism and fascism exist, football stadiums are also used as arenas by conflicting political ideologies, but in a far more explicitly political way than in Britain. Also, the NF and BM anti-immigrant position and predominantly young working-class support make them quite distinctive among contemporary European far-right groups. In France the Front National and the Parti des Forces nouvelles found that anti-migrant-worker appeals fell on deaf young ears. The Nederlandse Folksunie in Holland did have more success whipping up young workers against Surinam immigrants, but got itself banned in 1978.

# Portrait of a Racist

Decent, law-abiding citizens, who still believe that England is basically a tolerant country, are definitely in for a shock if they ever meet Barry Watts. Bull-necked and shaven-headed, decked out in leather belt, boots and braces, a bewildering array of tattoos cover his muscular arms (he's a body-building fanatic): MOTHER, JULIET, WEST HAM UNITED, ENGLAND, WHITE POWER. On his skull is scrawled SKINHEAD, and on his cheek, immediately below the eye is etched a small swastika.

Barry likes what he sees in the mirror. He feels his appearance adds to his manliness and he fancies his chances as a professional 'bird-puller'. But his confidence in his hardness is only skin deep. He prefers to go around with a group of white mates for protection, he says, against 'the blacks'. He's twenty-one and lives with his mum and dad on a run-down high-rise estate in the East End of London. He is near phobic about leaving his immediate neighbourhood.

A school failure, unskilled and constantly in trouble with the law, Barry's job prospects, like those of so many of his generation, are pretty dismal. Once he was a kitchen porter in a local hospital. Now he spends his days looking for black kids half his age to 'hospitalize'. Evenings, he and his mates patrol the forbidding streets around Mile End, looking to set on Asian workers coming home from nearby factories, or daubing walls with racist slogans. To unemployed lads like this, the graffiti NF doesn't just mean National Front but NO FUTURE.

Barry may act like a stereotype fascist, but his life and experiences are filled with contradictions. He loves reggae music, for example, and can understand the *patois*, which he picked up from West Indian kids at school. He once had a close mate who was black and he still uses 'rude boy' slang, if only to crack racist jokes among his friends. He wasn't always a Nazi. Some years ago, following a 'Rock

116

against Racism' gig where he went to hear his favourite reggae band, Steel Pulse, he had a brief flirtation with some comrades from the Socialist Workers Party ('Skins against the Nazis'), but soon left in disgust when he found he was being treated as a pet-mascot convert. His interest in politics remained undimmed, however. He joined the National Front shortly afterwards. Yet even here, although attracted by the Front's reputation as 'the violent party' or 'the hatred party', this wasn't the whole story: 'We're for the old folks, we're for them. We think they should get a better deal. And for the kiddies, somewhere for them to play. Better schools.' Why then won't he vote Labour like his parents and grandparents? 'Labour's only in it for themselves.' Besides, he holds them responsible for immigration. Yet he also hates the Tories, the rich, the police and authority in general.

Recently, however, Barry has got fed up with the 'respectable racism' of the NF, their miserable showing in elections and all the subsequent party splits. So now he follows the even more explicitly Nazi and violent British Movement. He'll readily admit, though, that the chances of any extreme-right group getting to power are slight, and his own personal prospects he sees as just as bleak: 'I can't even afford to go to the away matches with West Ham.' Yet one thing he is positive about. He wants his children to grow up feeling 'British and proud of it', and that means not being afraid to do a hard day's work, not being dependent on charity and not being afraid to stand up for yourself in a fight: 'Bomb the Argentine!' And, if he died tomorrow, what would he like as his epitaph? 'An East End lad born and bred'. But the BM are Nazis, and the Nazis bombed the East End to the ground. 'I know we fought a war against 'em. But Hitler to me is like Napoleon was to you. Nazis ... it puts *fear* into people.'

In the summer of 1982, the England national team took part in the World Cup Final in Spain. Barry and his mates went along with them 'to fly the flag'.

# Satellite City

Changes in a working-class neighbourhood happen slowly. People who have lived in an area all their lives will talk about the changes they have seen. But only in hindsight. Changes are only clearly visible on looking back. At the time it is hard to tell whether the changes you feel going on around you are real or just the products of your imagination. Sometimes a combination of real and imagined changes can profoundly alter the whole moral outlook of a community.

The South Afton estate in West London is a large public high-rise housing development. Building started after the war and has continued ever since. The estate replaced an old neighbourhood which had contained the elements of a strong occupational community based on domestic laundries. When these businesses went into virtual extinction in the sixties, they were replaced by light electronics and food-processing plants located on a new industrial estate. The rigid separation between working and living areas created large barren spaces. The absence of street life made lifts, stairs and walkways unwelcoming and unsafe at night. There was nowhere among the growing number of grey, anonymous concrete blocks for people to meet. However, a minute away was the old Victorian High Street, whose busy shops, pubs, cinemas and department stores had been left untouched by the planners. But its traditional character was changing. By the end of the sixties most of the old shops and properties around the High Street had been settled by Asian and West Indian families. Some were being rehoused on the estate itself.

By the mid-seventies many tenants felt that the prices of goods and services were not the only things that were getting out of hand. In a single month in 1976, they claimed, a newly installed chain of phone booths had been wrecked, a popular elderly couple were attacked and robbed, someone had covered the walls with obscene graffiti, and an outbreak of cat strangling was reported.

People felt angry and neglected. There were calls for more police patrols, and widespread disillusionment with the Labour-controlled Council in this solid Labour-voting ward. Some tenants went further. They imagined they could see a definite pattern between the area's history and this latest fragmented series of incidents. When, a few months later, the old municipal Town Hall, that symbol of Victorian propriety, was closed down, then 'taken over' by a West Indian community group and converted into a drop-in centre for black youth, their suspicions seemed to them to be confirmed.

In 1977, following a series of purse-snatching incidents in the High Street, the South Afton Tenants Association petitioned the Council for the black youth centre, the Venue, to be closed down. Yet the language of this tenants' protest was never openly racist. Instead, they presented the closure of the Venue as just one part of a full-scale 'clean-up campaign to discourage crime and vandalism and to restore the good name of our estate'.

Among parents, racism took the form of a defence of respectability; among their children it took the form of a defence of territory. There were regular skirmishes with black youth who had come from all over London to attend live 'reggae nites' at the Venue.

By the spring of 1977, when I visited the area, local youth provision had polarized entirely on racial lines. If whites felt out of place in the Venue, blacks were being made to feel more uncomfortable in the Proud Youth Centre, a shabby converted primary school near by. However, this did not mean that the Proud clientele displayed homogeneity of interests. In the Proud two distinct groups stood out. The first group was a small band of fifteen- to nineteen-year-olds, girls and boys, dressed as punks. School truants, dole-queue rockers, they coalesced around a charismatic eighteen-year-old, Denis Grant, editor of his own punk fanzine, *Westway*, and lead-singer and founder-member of The Satellites: 'It's because we live in Satellite City. We're cut off from the rest of the world stuck out on this estate.' The other main grouping consisted of a hard core of half a dozen teenage boys and lots of school-age hangers-on. Broken homes, failure at school, trouble with the Law, formed their collective background. Some had recently joined the National Front and had become known as the Afton Mafia.

A typical evening in the club: in one room, Grant struggling with a wonky old duplicator to get out the latest issue of *Westway*; next door, the Afton Mafia patiently folding and collating copies of *Bulldog* and other racist literature. On one occasion I was asked if I had read Lady Birdwood's pamphlet 'Choice: The Case for Repatriation'. Strongly recommended! Was this evidence of how territorial gang-rivalry had spawned a grassroots fascist political culture? Not so long ago, left groups such as the Young Communist League and YCND (Young Campaign for Nuclear Disarmament) had branches in this neighbourhood. Jazz and folk music evenings, poetry readings, as well as demonstrations and newspaper selling activities such as these had provided a kind of counter-society of fellowship, reason and purpose, mainly for those looking upward and outward from the neighbourhood, with O- and A-level tickets to ride, but also for some working youth. That these organizations had been able to get established at all had been due to the efforts of a few dedicated socialist families who lived locally and did not share the prevailing pessimism that regarded new estates as political wildernesses. Their places in the political landscape had been taken in the mid-seventies by a former Council cleansing department worker who had stood for the National Front in the 1976 GLC elections. Encouraged by the support he received from white youth in his campaign, he had set about organizing a branch of the Young National Front. An inaugural all-white disco was announced: no reggae or soul music allowed. (As it turned out, the disco proved abortive, poorly attended and it ended ignominiously in scuffles – 'white on white' – and with the police being called.)

But being in the YNF was not really about joining a political party branch, or changing one's musical preferences from Stevie Wonder to Glen Campbell. Rather, it signalled a move from territory-based gang war towards the beginning of a sustained and quite paranoid campaign of racial intimidation on the streets. Asian children coming home from school were favourite targets.

The Proud punks, on the other hand, appeared disinterested in such calculated thuggery. However, their cultural pursuits, and those of the Afton Mafia, were not entirely mutually exclusive. Being self-consciously punk, Grant's fanzine, *Westway*, abounded in sado-masochistic images culled from modern pornography, and these included Nazi uniforms, swastikas, jackboots, etc. The fascination with the Nazi era in popular culture was one of the signs of the times in the late seventies. Previously, talk of Hitler and concentration camp horrors had been confined to the illicit realms of the profane, censored out of classrooms, youth clubs and most homes. Now it provided a vital, sexually provocative ingredient in youth culture. Fascism had become fashionable, sexy. Some of the punks had even voted NF in 1976 'because we thought it was the trendy thing to do'. Swastikas on the drum-kit, '*sieg heil*' chants from the terraces – all part of the iconography of contemporary youth culture. Countless thousands, including very young children, have been drawn to this popular, outrageous and shocking element in youth culture.

However, playing with the images of Nazism is a long way from the hard-core racist position of the Afton Mafia. What distinguished them from their contemporaries was that they all lived out their racism irrespective of where they were or who they were with. When Glen McGrath, aged seventeen, was injured in a fight and had to go to hospital, he refused to be treated by a coloured nurse or doctor 'even if it means I bleed to death'. When Terry Ladd, aged seventeen, got a job in a small print shop and was asked to join a union, he refused on the grounds that the shop steward was an Asian. No union card, no work. Carl Wood, normally well-behaved and sociable at school, had unhesitatingly backed up a National-Front-inspired hate campaign against a supposed 'Red teacher', and had been expelled for it. In the following interview these boys tell of the conspiracy their adult mentors have encouraged them to feel they are up against. But first they describe how they petitioned white residents of the estate following on mob action to defend their territory.

*'You got into a fight the other night. What happened?'*

CARL: Well, there was a fair fight between one of my brothers and this coloured kid, right; and they started one on to one, and they [the blacks] said it was all over. But all that week, every night after this place[1] closed, they all come down, about forty or fifty of them, from all over – Shepherd's Bush, Notting Hill, White City.
GLEN: Black City! [*Laughter.*]

1. The Proud Youth Centre.

121

TERRY: And there was just our lot here, from our estate.

CARL: Even the older blokes came out of their houses, didn't they?
There was older people coming out of their houses when they seen
all the white kids getting nicked – they were going mad about it!
Because they seen what happened.

TERRY: And we got up a petition.

GLEN: Yes, we just went round the houses and we said to the people,
you know, 'Why was we getting nicked?', and they just signed their
names. We got about a hundred names in three days.

*'So the white people on the estate were sympathetic?'*

CARL: Yes.

GLEN: Because they seen all the trouble from their balconies.

CARL: Everyone was looking over their balconies; there was a big
audience. *Everyone* was out!

TERRY: Some of the older blokes came out, and they started fighting
as well. [*Laughter*.] One bloke came down from the flats with just
a pair of trousers on and a vest and he started fighting. [*Laughter*.]

*'Are most of the people on this estate white?'*

TERRY: *Half* of them are, yes; not most of them. It used to be –
didn't it? – white. Now it's about half and half; half black and half
white.

*'In this fight did all the black kids come from outside the area?'*

GLEN: All from outside the area. Well, *one* lived here, but all the rest
came from outside.

*'Would you have gone outside your area to fight?'*

GLEN: I wouldn't, personally. You see, if we went outside our area . . .
Remember when we got nicked? The police said, 'If you're on your
own territory we'll nick the others, but if you're outside it we'll nick
you.' So we let them come down to us. And on the Friday night
we was fetching bottles and sticks and everything and we hid them,
and the Old Bill come and they found them all and they nicked us,
and we got done for conspiracy to cause GBH. Nine of us got
done.

CARL: But I mean, the blacks come down for us, right? And there was

more of them that what there was of us. So we had to collect
bottles and that to defend ourselves.

TERRY: The thing that got them worked up was that the cops got
some blacks one night, and they let them go down town.

GLEN: Yes, on the night before we got nicked, the cops put them
in the back of the meat wagon, right, and they took them back
up to town and dropped them off. So they let them go. Just sent
them back to their area. But they nicked us.

*'Why do you think they let them go?'*

GLEN: Race relations, I think ... Race Relations Act, whatever they
call it. If they get nicked, they go on all that Race Relations Board
stuff; they start complaining, saying the police are nicking them
unfairly, picking them up.

TERRY: That was in the *Gazette*– they were picking them up on 'sus'
or something – suspicion to do things. And they actually caught
them doing it! But they let them go. But they nicked us lot.

CARL: They were the ones who'd come down; they had sticks and
everything! And the police seen it. They even caught them with
sticks and everything in their hands, didn't they? And they let them
go!

*'So you think the police are biased against white people?'*

CARL: No, they're not biased against white people; they're biased
against *us*! They know really quite a few of us – don't they? – and if
they see you they nick you. But if they see a bunch of black kids
hanging about, they wouldn't nick them.

TERRY: That used to happen nearly every day round our area: we
used to get searched. They used to come over if you're in a group –
like the week before we got nicked, remember? If you hang about
after ten o'clock, a copper come over and he said to me, 'If you lot
ain't out of here in five minutes you're nicked, the lot of you.'

GLEN: Any fighting round our area which involves blacks and whites,
they'll let the blacks go. I've seen it, even years ago, when the
bigger lads used to fight. I actually seen a lad getting whacked in
front of our flat by a black kid, and I saw they caught him, and
let him go and nicked the other lad. The police have been doing it
all the time round our way.

TERRY: Yes, there used to be a bigger lot round here, you know, like eighteen, nineteen. Now they're off and married, so *we* hang about and we get the trouble.

GLEN: Down our way they pick on white mostly, nearly all the time they would.

*'You have all grown up round here. How would you describe this area?'*

CARL: It was good when we were smaller; it was much better, wasn't it?

TERRY: Yes.

GLEN: Where our flats are, all it is now are green and trees and everything; there used to be rubbish dumps and mud and all that, and we used to have a laugh there. You know what I mean.

CARL: There used to be a lot of older houses, and we all used to go in them. But they've been knocking everything down. We can't even have a bonfire round our way now – can we? – without them phoning the police.

GLEN: Now we've got *one* club down there, and that ain't much of a club either – it's falling down. [*Laughter.*] It's got a post in the middle holding the ceiling up! And that's the only club. Well, there is a new one, but they won't open it. A brand new club, and they use it for old people; bingo and that.

TERRY: A year ago, right, we was in there; we went in there for a meeting, right, and this bloke's going, 'Yes, we'll have boxing, weightlifting, everything.' Next thing we know, old pensioners are using it in the daytime, and that's it! It's closed now.

CARL: They just keep on building flats, don't they? They're opening a new lot now at the top of the road there. It just keeps on getting bigger and bigger – this estate. It's nearly one of the biggest in London now.

GLEN: And how many houses have gone to blacks in just them two blocks already?

TERRY: They should build little houses, you know. Small blocks of flats.

GLEN: Even when we went on holiday to the Isle of Wight, some people had heard the reputation of our estate. On holiday! Unbelievable!

CARL: Yes, we all went to the Isle of Wight – about twenty of us, wasn't it? We was down at the seaside and that, and these people come from outside London, and we talked to them, and they asked where we come from, and we said South Afton, and they said, 'Oh, that's a rough place, ain't it!'

GLEN: London is a drag. [*Laughter.*] It is! I ain't joking. I mean, you live out in the country and you can have the time of your life. But when you're stuck in a hole like this ...! We're like baked beans in a tin can. [*Laughter.*] There's nothing to do down our way; you can't even play football!

*'You said last time we met that you had all joined the National Front ...?*

CARL: Yes.

TERRY: Yes!

GLEN: I'm not a member, but I've been to marches and meetings with them.

TERRY: And my mate Jerry's a member; and that other bloke, John.

CARL: No, he's not; he's just two-faced. [*Laughter.*] Like, when he's with, say, just us lot and my brother, he's going on about the National Front. But when he's with someone who don't like the National Front, he starts on about it; he starts saying, 'No, nor do I,' and things like that.

*'Does being in the National Front help solve the problems of your estate?'*

CARL: You're saying that we're in the National Front just to get rid of the blacks and keep our estate white. That's what you're trying to say, ain't it?

*'Well, are black people really the problem?'*

CARL: Well, er ...

TERRY: They cause all the muggings of old women and that.

GLEN: I was walking down the street with Kentucky and chips. I walked past some of them and I didn't have Kentucky and chips [*Laughter*] and that's true! I'd have the guts to go and nick someone's Kentucky and chips – but I wouldn't *do* it. But *they* do. They'd nick anything.

TERRY: The National Front's the only party that'll do anything about it, I reckon.

125

*'About what?'*

TERRY: About coloureds, about black people.

CARL: They've got other policies and all. Like getting us out of the Common Market and all this ... Stopping the IRA. They want to bring back capital punishment for terrorists and all this – I reckon their ideas are all right. They ain't Fascists or anything like that.

TERRY: *Sieg heil!* [*Laughter.*]

Eventually their extremism drove me to extremes. A battle of class-thinking against race-thinking ensued: from them, Powellite fantasies of rivers of blood; from me, heroic armed workers taking over key-points in the city in the struggle for socialism. Alarmingly, the logic of both sides' arguments was the same: *civil war*. The trouble was that when driven into a corner I found it hard to supply convincing human targets for class hatred. The boys also preferred to focus their hatred on *powerless* groups in society: blacks, gays, SS scroungers, Boat People, squatters, as well as police and bosses. In fact, truly powerful people may not be popular, but at least they have a function. A factory needs its managers; a soccer club needs its board of directors. And such people are seldom the *main* cause of popular resentment. Rather, it is wealth without visible function that is really hated – 'rich Jews', 'that coloured geezer with a big flash car'. Such people are seen as parasites on the honest labour of working people.

Confronting the underlying issues of power and powerlessness is a central task for political education in schools. But working-class students will not be won over from the irrational to an alternative political idealism by the waving of red flags and by exhortations. As survivors of the youth revolution of the sixties learnt, in politics idealism is frequently no more than an excuse for not recognizing unpleasant realities. Idealism can be a form of evading reality altogether.

It has to be admitted that political and multi-cultural education programmes would do little to curb the fantasies of committed racists such as the Afton Mafia. Just as it is unlikely that being exposed to such strategies at an early age would have made much difference to the political development of a Goebbels, or that multi-cultural courses in Judaism would have deterred many from joining the Hitler

Youth. The task of educators is limited to producing enough politically and morally educated people capable of taking up the fight against their racist contemporaries. The real anti-racist struggle lies within the peer group, as the following incident reveals.

Impressed by Johnny Rotten's pronouncement on Capital Radio that 'No one should be a fascist. In fact it's wrong, totally wrong', Denis Grant, the leader of the local punks, decided to intervene in my argument with the Afton Mafia. He had been to school with them, had got to know them quite well. 'But I never reckoned this lot, ever.' There followed some calculated abuse about their alleged lack of grey matter. Ignoring threats of dire bodily injury, Grant went on to tell how they had been thrown out of a disco. The manager had objected to their NF badges and requested them to remove the offensive articles. They had characteristically refused and were forced to make a humiliating exit. Next day they were harassed and eventually set upon by some black schoolgirls, after attempting to distribute 'Smash the Red Teachers' leaflets outside a comprehensive school. In everyday life, then, hard-core racists are forced to make a choice – between becoming lonely, embittered social outcasts, at home only in the far-right company of batty old women and seedy-looking men, if they hold their racist positions; or to change their ways if they want to be accepted in a multi-racial society.

As for the Afton Mafia, it is highly likely that before that day arrives, if it ever does, their street crimes will lead them to a long stretch in prison. (Shortly after I visited them, police raided a disused garage and found Molotov cocktails and other materials to make primitive explosive devices.) Inside, they will meet many prisoners, and some prison officers, who will tell them that they have been locked up, not as dangerous thugs but as political prisoners, fighters for a new fascist order 'to save old England from decline'. One fascist street song runs:

> He was only a poor little skinhead
> He wandered alone in the night
> Now he's joined the National Front
> And he's found a reason to fight.

# The Kids United

The huge Anti-Nazi League and 'Rock against Racism' rallies and concerts of the late seventies were intended to show that for every racist there were thousands who opposed racialism and welcomed the realities of the multi-racial society.

The main medium for the anti-racist message was music. In the sixties rock was the burning issue among the young, but apart from the emergence of reggae the early seventies was a period of decline, at least in terms of innovation and creativity (the profits from record sales continued to rise). The best the music industry could come up with had been glamrock. As performed by David Bowie or Gary Glitter it projected an image of hard lads dressed up to the nines in high heels, elaborate make-up – and a set of tattoos. A deliberately cultivated decadence – New York gay meets thirties Berliner, with the pose becoming less pretty and more Nazi. But when the glitter wore off glitterock there was little left.

The appearance of punk rock in the late seventies may have owed less to glamrock and more to the conceptual art movement that was sweeping the art schools. However, punk's 'sound and vision' was far less esoteric than that suggests. With their maudlin lyrics and tinkling chord-sequences, most seventies pop musicians were still busy roaming Hippy Hill. In contrast, punk was direct and anti-emotional; the lack of subtlety and extreme technical limitations of some bands even recalled fifties skiffle. Except that, as I have already mentioned, Iron Crosses and swastikas were also involved – there was much self-conscious dabbling in fascist images of sex and power. But then things began to get out of hand. At punk gigs the growth of racism eventually gave many musicians a new sense of moral responsibility.[1] Bands such as The Clash, The Specials and Sham 69

1. In sharp contrast to the racist remarks of some rock superstars.

donated their services free to 'Rock against Racism'. By the end of the decade they had attained a massive following among youth of all classes, while among working-class boys music, rather than football, was capturing the imagination. Denis Grant was a recent defector from the soccer scene:

'I have lost interest in football. I think a lot of people have. It's just – boring. The players seem a million miles away from the kids. They might come from the same backgrounds, but they earn so much money, they're superstars. They would piss on us if they had the chance.

'I suppose ten years ago you had to have some sort of escape, and, well, what was there? The hippies? That was all put on. Hippies were middle-class, I reckon, except for the more gipsy types. They were all right. But the rest of the hippie business was very false. [*Mimics*] "Yeah, man! It's really far out, man! Pass the spiff, man!" It was just put on. All that peace and love shit which no one believes any more, cos it don't work.

'So I suppose football catered for a lot of working-class people. A place where *they* could get together. But now music has taken over as the main escape. It's so much easier to be in a punk rock band or do a punk mag than it is to be another Bobby Charlton. You have to be really great to be a footballer – though you do get shitty footballers. But to form a band you don't have to be that great. That's what most professional musicians put it down for. But it's good rock 'n' roll, right? Like the rock 'n' roll in the fifties, with the teddy boys, before the hippies came along and made it all middle-class. It don't matter that some bands can't hold down *that* chord perfectly. Nobody really cares if "he's not got 'is augmented ninth down perfect".

'The song lyrics – they're all about being on the dole, living on estates, white riot, real things like this. It's better than all those hippie songs about "We're all going to Mars". I reckon this whole rock movement, "Rock against Racism", punks, reggae – it was to fill a void in the kids' lives. The football supporters are the potential audience. A lot of the bands, like Sham 69, have got packs of skin-heads following 'em around, like they used to follow football teams. They go around everywhere with the groups.'

*'And they have fights with rival fans?'*

'They do, but it's not so much. A lot of 'em *are* in the Nazi parties. But the ones who really go out to fight, they can go to a disco and fight. There's a hell of a lot of stabbings at discos now. There's not so much rivalry between punk fans really. There was a battle with the teds in the King's Road, but that was nothing much. It's not so much against each other. At football you get the Stretford End and the Shed fighting each other when really they should be with each other. Like Sham 69 sing, "The kids united will never be defeated!"'

Nevertheless, the dangerous confusions and contradictions that young people carry in their heads, not only about racism but about politics in general, remained. The 1977 Anti-Nazi League march against the National Front from Trafalgar Square to a rock festival in Victoria Park attracted a crowd of one hundred thousand. That included skinhead NF sympathizers. If not to cause trouble, why had they gone? 'They wanted to hear the reggae band, Steel Pulse, didn't they?' White skins had long been impressed by the vitality and dynamism of black music, as well as by the fighting prowess of black youth. (This was in contrast to Asian youth who possess no comparable musical or street-gang traditions and who get singled out as special targets for hatred by black *and* white.)

Many whites happily followed two-tone, reggae/ska-influenced bands such as The Specials and still believed it best to 'send the blacks home'. In skinhead circles, where they were especially popular, this band was known as The Specials Plus-Two, referring to the two black members of the group.

At the other extreme, some anti-racists, wearing CND badges, also sport bigger and better Doc Martens! The experience of attending a tough comprehensive, coupled with the knowledge that good exam results no longer automatically lead to a good job, has led large sections of middle-class youth to pursue a path of downward social mobility, actively to identify with the aggressive combative *posture* of working-class youth, while at the same time rejecting the underlying racist and sexist attitudes. These 'toy skins' and 'toy punks', as they are sometimes referred to by their more sceptical contemporaries, opted for a macho response to working-class racism which found its most popular expression in the crude street-confrontation tactics favoured by left groups in the ANL, such as the Socialist Workers Party. The struggle against racism and other complex political questions are reduced to simpler and more familiar youthful scenarios of violent mob rivalry – the Reds up against the Nazis and so on.[2]

By the 1980s 'No one is really too sure what is happening ... Fascist skins, left-wing skins, and yet more skins who just like the clothes and the music.'[3] What next? Black skins and white Rastas? Endless permutations, endless gyrations: in Glasgow, Punks Rule; in East London, the skins; in Birmingham and the West End the nightclub-based new romantics movement, whose main activity involves dressing-up in extravagant gear – an extreme form of narcissistic self-involvement with no connection with anything outside itself – 'It's like living inside a Fred Astaire movie during the depression.' All over the country, but especially in the big northern cities, 'heavy metal' holds sway. These are generally peace-loving and non-aggressive followers of ultra-loud neo-hippie rock bands such as Thin Lizzie and Saxon. Then there are the hybrid cults: psychobillys, half-skin half-rocker; Crocs and Casuals, forms of recherché mod. The message of the 1980s youth culture is: 'Choose your cult and live inside it.' Forget the rest.

Meanwhile cynical commercial interests encourage the young to go on chasing the trappings of affluence in yesterday's life-styles amidst the hardening realities of unemployment, racism and recession. Fortunately the politics of youth culture and the ethics of the football End have not entirely taken over! Many teachers and youth-workers still manage to build on what young people have in common, rather than emphasizing those aspects of their culture that divide them.

2. Indeed, the tendency of nation states to settle territorial disputes by violent means, and with only the slenderest of references to ideals or moral principles, can be read by the politically illiterate as no more than a grown-up version of soccer warfare. After the Malvinas dispute of 1982 (against soccer arch-rivals, Argentina, who an England soccer manager once called 'animals'), the young fans sang, 'Argentine, Argentine, what's it like to lose a war?'

3. Ian Walker in *New Society*, 26 June 1980.

Ray Quarless, a youth-worker from Liverpool 8 (Toxteth), describes the situation after a period of growing racial tension: 'People in Liverpool 8 said, "Let's get all the black kids and put them on this side, and get all the white kids and put them on that side, and then we can bring them together at the bridge." And that is what has happened in Liverpool. A lot of black kids have gone for the Rastafarian religion because they are rejecting what they learn in the formal education system. I am talking about 13- or 14-year-olds who don't go to school any more, but are completely attached to Rasta culture. They reject the society around them and have formed their own society in Liverpool 8. But the remarkable thing is that the white kids, they listen to the black kids now. They don't react now to black kids as they have done in the past, when they were calling them wogs and coons and niggers. There has been a sort of integration of the white kids with the black kids, which has happened at the same time as Rastafarianism has been going on as well. The black kids have not drawn them into their culture, of course, but into a relationship; not necessarily a brotherly relationship, but more just as human beings, aware of each other as black and white. In Liverpool 8, black and white kids *do* get along together.'

In the summer of 1981 this tentative alliance was put to the test, although, sadly, in a negative way, when black and white alike in Liverpool 8 took to the streets *en masse* to confront 'the single common enemy of the whole age group, the police'.

# Up against the Law

'It's the 1980s now ... Gangs roaming at will, burning down
police stations ... The whole of England's one giant pinball table.
The ball running wild.'

Howard Brenton, *Revenge* (1982)

If they have achieved nothing else, the riots that swept Britain's cities
in the summer of 1981 (and which have erupted sporadically and
with less publicity ever since), have managed fully to revive the great
public debate of the youth problem. The Prime Minister herself
kicked off. Her government had recently been elected on a strong
law and order ticket to deter juvenile offenders. At the height of
the disorders, she hurried from a garden party to address a bemused
and anxious nation.

Margaret Thatcher put the blame for the disturbances firmly on
the parents for failing to exercise a proper restraining influence over
their children. This was sadly ironic, when for thirty years parents
in working-class areas have been blaming each other: 'It's not my
kids, it's the ones next door who go around in gangs and get in
trouble.' Then one night little Johnny is driven home in the back
of a police car – a traumatic experience.

For the right-wing spokesman on race, Enoch Powell, the events
proved the impossibility of a multi-racial society, and were the fulfil-
ment of his nightmare vision of 'rivers of blood': 'I told you so.'
This assumption – that these were in effect race riots – was quickly
denied by the Home Secretary, the appropriately named William
Whitelaw. It was true that black youth were in the forefront of the
rioting, as they had been previously in the ghetto neighbourhoods
of Brixton, Notting Hill and St Paul's, Bristol. And in areas with
large Asian communities, such as Southall and Bradford, the disorders stemmed directly from threatened and attempted invasions
by gangs of white racist skinheads. However, such incidents were
very much a sub-text to the main drama. In the Liverpool 8 district
and in Moss Side, Manchester, large numbers of white youngsters
were actively involved in some of the fiercest rioting. Unfortunately
for the right-wing press only a tiny handful could be described as

133

Trotskyist troublemakers acting on orders from the revolutionary party.

Nevertheless a common response of many liberal commentators was to make direct comparisons with the explosions that shook the black ghettos of the United States in the sixties. Yet these took place against a great nationwide movement for civil rights, and were a reflection of a growing impatience with *promises* of political change. In Britain, by contrast, it was only *after* the riots, and the publication of the report on Lord Scarman's inquiry, that public debate switched from an insidious numbers game played around immigration to a recognition of the predicament of black people struggling to make their way in a racist society. Finally, for those observers with a knowledge of English history, the riots represented nothing new or unexpected. Rather, they were the continuation of a *tradition*. From the rick-burners and anti-Catholic mobs of the nineteenth century to anti-fascist disturbances in the East End in the thirties, riot and commotion is a necessary safety-valve, the best guarantee against the possibility of genuine revolutionary change, for riots are invariably the prelude to peaceful reform through parliament. The safety-valvists' case was strengthened when, from scenes of burning buildings and looted shops, the television screens were filled with delirious crowds celebrating the Royal Wedding. Yet for all their historical perspective, the safety-valvists could shed little light on the immediate causes of the troubles, nor could they explain the age and class specificity of most of the participants. So why had it happened? Some Labour politicians talked of a spontaneous revolt against unemployment and bad housing.

If you asked the young people involved, only one answer came back loud and clear: 'Reasons for riots? No matter where you go, to any part of the country, all kids think the same. They just hate coppers. They got no respect, they don't respect anybody, so you don't respect them, that's why. You get arrested. Kids in cells with yer, just been beaten up by coppers. They all say, "We'll get them coppers back for that." They just drag you about, coppers. All kids wanna get 'em back one day. Well, they got 'em back, didn't they?' (Sean, aged seventeen, Leeds United fan.)

In the folklore of working-class youth, the police are depicted as devils incarnate. On the soccer terrace, police sorties into the crowd to eject fighting fans would be greeted with chants of 'Kill, kill, kill the Bill!' In 1968 a man who murdered two police officers, went on the run, and was eventually captured and sentenced to life imprisonment, became a folk hero to skinhead soccer fans.

> Harry Roberts is our friend
> He kills coppers
> Put him on the streets again
> Let him kill some others
> Harry Roberts is our friend
> HE KILLS COPPERS!

For most kids the events of 1981 were less a matter of protest against unemployment, more a summer version of soccer warfare with the police as the main target: 'In winter we come up against 'em on terraces, in summer on the streets.' The speed with which the riots spread was fresh evidence of the existence of a whole youth under-life, with everyday links in schools, playgrounds, pubs, cafés and discotheques, which were now alive with rumours of fresh fronts being opened up, and prisons being emptied to make room for captured insurgents. Gangs would converge on troubled areas from all parts of the city and sometimes beyond, as they do on soccer grounds.

This was the culmination of thirty years' bitter struggle based on the question: Who rules round here? Kids or cops? As Frankie Rice, North London skinhead, recalled: 'We have a lot of trouble with the Law. We have fights with them all the time. They pick us up for nothing. We would be walking across the street and they would say, "Oi! You! Come 'ere!", get us in the back of the cop car and give us a bit of a kickin' down the cop shop, and then let us go, cos they had nothing on us, did they? It used to happen once a week, twice a week. They just wanted to keep us in our place.'

In some neighbourhoods, clashes with the police are not confined to the young but involve the entire community. As the Liverpool 8 Defence Group point out: 'Relationships with the police and the local community in Liverpool 8 have never been easy, and in recent years have deteriorated to such a level that they must be considered a principal cause of the outbreaks in summer 1981. There have been many allegations of police harassment over several years and members of the community often feel that the police are against them rather than acting on their behalf.'

Elsewhere, a more familiar picture is of young people isolated in their communities, harassed by the police, while their parents strive for respectability and, rather than supporting their children, support calls for greater police stop-and-search powers and harsher sentences. Black youth have felt particularly isolated and exposed to harassment from racist elements within the police. In areas with a strong black youth presence, police swamp operations aimed at deterring street crime. Their actions are intended to threaten the livelihood of the hustler, the dope-dealer and the petty thief. They also threaten the freedom to stand around and do nothing.

As Lord Scarman reported, police efforts to intervene to rescue injured victims of gang rivalry are also firmly resisted (as at football grounds, where the kids fight the Law after police attempt to stop them fighting each other). And if the conflict escalates to the point where the police suddenly find themselves outnumbered and on the defensive, then there are rich pickings to be had for those who want the goods (TV, hi-fi, etc.), but *now*, with no down-payment. (Looting has its ironies. A community-worker in Brixton tries to dissuade some kids from looting a jeweller's shop: 'This our gold, man! It come from South Africa!')

Some police officers will privately defend their rough treatment of juveniles, pointing out that 'If parents or teachers won't discipline them, and keep them in line, then it is up to us.' In full-scale street riots, with resources severely stretched, the police – forced to suffer heavy casualties – dropped all pretence of being *in loco parentis*, and went out of control, just as the kids had done. In Brixton officers in plain clothes were observed wielding pickaxe handles to make their point.

To senior police officers such as James Anderton, chief constable of Manchester, the urban youth mob is bracketed with the IRA as Enemies of the People. According to Anderton, here quoted in the *Guardian*, the job of the police is no less than to defend the values of western Christian democratic society against these modern equivalents of the 'dangerous classes' of the nineteenth century: 'Rampaging, drunken and violent hooligans who roam the city streets, crash through our shops and stores, cause damage and wreak havoc wherever they go, and implant fear in the stoutest hearts among us, are surely not deserving of much save severe condemnation and'harsh punishment. Marauding gangs of dirty youth ... defiantly chanting the crudest obscenities, have no right to be regarded as rational, responsible people; rather they should expect to bear the yoke of a public penalty made heavy by the anger their own uncivilized behaviour evokes.'

Such sentiments are not welcomed by the liberal political establishment or by more enlightened police officers. Following the Scarman Report there appears to be a growing realization, even in conservative circles, that the youth problem is not solely a problem of law enforcement; rather it is how to give young people a stake in society as productive workers and responsible citizens. For the young this means that the answer lies not in street riots, or the latest convolution of youth culture, but in that nasty, grown-up political world which most kids 'don't give a toss' about, and few feel very confident about dealing with.

After the riots, the government promised more money for the inner cities and for youth-training initiatives. But the convictions resulting from the 1981 disturbances have expanded the prison population to record levels, while the continuation of Margaret Thatcher's economic policies is creating a new generation of criminals. In Brixton in 1981 a youth-worker surveyed the smoking wreckage: 'That's ten years of youth and community work up in smoke! Things will calm down for a while, but it's too late for reforms now. Even if the government changed tomorrow, and there was more money, lots more, it won't really help. It will all be too late ...'

# In and Out of Work

Work experience?
We have no work.
Work experience?
Don't make us laugh.
You'll count the cost.
You'll reap the harvest of the lost;
You'll experience.

Bernard Kops, *Missing Out*

Without any help from the police or soccer clubs, the economic winds
are blowing away the Chelsea Shed. The majority of those who go
to football and stand up the Ends tend to be concentrated at the
lower end of the twelve to twenty-four age range. But what of those
who have left school and are 'senior' figures in the End hierarchy?
What kind of jobs are they most commonly in? To find out I con-
structed a sample from the Chelsea Shed 1968–78, using interviews,
local newspaper reports of soccer offenders, and comprehensive
police records of persons ejected from the ground but not subse-
quently charged with any criminal offence. Shedboy jobs prominent
in my sample included: scaffolder, butcher's boy, labourer, van boy,
factory-hand, electrician's mate, gas fitter, packer, warehouseman,
coffin finisher, baker, Post Office trainee, brewery worker, storeman,
apprentice lithographer, housepainter, window-cleaner, plasterer,
apprentice toolmaker.

The variety of semi-skilled and unskilled manual work may show
the Dickensian, nineteenth-century nature of the youth labour
market in West London. But in another, smaller sample of 'official'
soccer hooligans aged sixteen to twenty-one who appeared at Highbury Magistrates Court in the 1974–5 season, much the same pattern
of employment arises: skilled non-manual, zero; skilled manual, five;
semi-skilled and unskilled (including temporarily unemployed),
thirty-six; apprentice/trainee, eleven.

The 'occupational mix' of the Arsenal North Bank is the same
as the Chelsea Shed – heavily biased towards the unskilled casual
end of the job market. In terms of the current crisis of youth employment, then, these boys form part of the most vulnerable section of

138

the workforce.[1] Customarily valued as cheap labour, as fetchers and carriers for bosses and foremen, they would often move from job to job in highly localized labour markets. Today small firms and businesses no longer find it necessary or profitable to employ un- skilled school-leavers. As Phil Cohen has pointed out: 'Continuous processes and double-shifts, new information technologies, ration- alization of labour, automation and the mechanization of fetching and carrying operations – all these developments ... have been so many nails in the coffin of youth labour ... The recession aggravates these factors, especially in the more backward sectors of the distribu- tion and service trades which traditionally took on unskilled school- leavers. But if a British economic miracle were to happen tomorrow, the displacement of youth labour would accelerate to more than counter-balance the absorption due to growth. Under a mixed economy, structural youth unemployment is here to stay ...'[2]

If the need to assert one's physical hardness is bound up with manual labour and earning a wage, then more and more future Shed- dites will be acting hard without access to hard work.

Of course, the current crisis does not only affect boys like this. Of the thousands of youngsters leaving school in the summer of 1982, some 80 per cent were without academic qualifications, and in some big cities scarcely one in five could be hopeful of finding secure employment. The scale of the crisis is not new; there is here a long history. But the *experience* of growing up working-class in the 1980s is very different from growing up in the 1930s or 1830s, or even, for that matter, from growing up in the 1960s.

Youth labour has always been one of the most exploited sections of the working class. In the thirties 80 per cent of children left school at the age of fourteen to form the mass of recruits to industry. The following picture by John Jewkes, the economist, is an adequate summary of their situation: 'In many parts of the country, notably the depressed Northern districts, the years between the ages of four- teen and eighteen ... have become years of sporadic employment, often in blind-alley occupations or in industries already overcrowded with adults; of interrupted training; of weary and deadening

1. They have this in common with black youth with whom they share the inner city and against whom they have to compete for employment in the locality.
2. From 'School for Dole' in *New Socialist*, January 1982.

idleness.'[3] This 'idleness', the mass unemployment of youth, was as much a new social phenomenon in the thirties as it is in our post-war society. In the nineteenth century, before the Factory Acts and the growth of the Labour organizations put an end to the worst excesses, the massive expansion of British industry was dependent on plentiful supplies of children and young people and their harsh exploitation.

In *Capital* (1867) Marx describes this process and foretells the logical development of the crisis of youth labour in the changing conditions of machinery and of factory production:

Both in the factories proper, and in the large workshops, where machinery enters as one factor, or even where no more than a division of labour of a modern type has been put into operation, large numbers of male workers are employed up to the age of maturity, but not beyond. Once they reach maturity, only a very small number continue to find employment in the same branches of industry, while the majority are regularly dismissed. This majority forms an element of the floating surplus population, which grows with the extension of those branches of industry. Some of these workers emigrate; in fact they are merely following capital, which has itself emigrated. A further consequence is that the female population grows more rapidly than the male – witness England. That the natural increase in the number of workers does not satisfy the requirements of the accumulation of capital, and yet, at the same time, exceeds those requirements, is a contradiction inherent in capital's very movement. Capital demands more youthful workers, fewer adults. The contradiction is not more glaring than the other contradiction, namely that a shortage of 'hands' is complained of, while, at the same time, many thousands are out of work, because the division of labour chains them to a particular branch of industry.[4]

As long as production expanded (not of course in a straight line but in ups and downs), so the movement of capital created places for the young and spurred their collective expectations of a better life. But beyond the high points of capitalist development, production could no longer absorb the youth; urban migration was one major response. But in the slumps in the British economy of the inter-war years, it became virtually impossible for youth to find a place in

3. John Jewkes and Allan Winterbottom, *Juvenile Unemployment*, Allen & Unwin, 1933.

4. Karl Marx, *Capital*, Volume 1, Penguin, 1976, p. 794.

any industry at anything approaching a decent wage. All hope of joining the basic stratum of adult workers had to be deferred. Instead a place in the huge standing army of young unemployed was guaranteed.

Here, I think, lies a clue to the power of football as a metaphor of the ups and downs of working-class life which follow on the booms and slumps of the capitalist system of production: its popular function as a barometer by which people can measure both the state of the nation and their own state. There is therefore always an added poignancy to the claim of an elderly supporter, who may have experienced several periods of redundancy in his working life, to have followed his favourite team through thick and thin. Today the volatility and yearning for spectacle and excitement of young soccer crowds has replaced the old-fashioned stoicisms of the inter-war generations. And not only when it comes to watching football. For the stoic response was learnt elsewhere, outside the ground. And what stoicism! Of the hundreds of thousands of young people made idle in those hungry years, very few ever received unemployment benefit. Many were herded into dole schools – the hated Belmonts. A spell in such primitive labour camps was supposed to prevent demoralization. Even the most exploitative of today's youth opportunities schemes would have seemed like a soft option by comparison.

The level of national health care was so wretched in those years that when thousands tried to join the army nearly two thirds were rejected as physically unfit.[5]

With nine out of ten of the potential youth labour-force completely unskilled and the doors to industrial training closed, there was a steady drift towards the new light repetition industries, into distribution – van boys and butcher's boys – into domestic service, to the parasitic pursuits – bookies' runners on street corners – and into petty crime. Such work opportunities escalated massively after the war and were to provide the basis of the semi-skilled and unskilled casual labour market in which the Chelsea Shedboys earned enough money to pay their entrance into the ground.

5. In the ten years from 1927 to 1937, 760,000 tried to join up. On health grounds 473,000 were rejected.

Another way in which unorganized working youth solved the problem of how to survive in the thirties was through urban migration. This was drift migration, less dangerous to other people's property than the life of the street preferred by today's urban youth. They took to the roads. 'It is impossible to measure the numbers of wandering youth, but they must run into tens of thousands scattered up and down the roads, sleeping in doss-houses or in the open, living in many cases on casual charity, in a never-ending search for work,' wrote John Gollan in *Youth in British Industry* (1936).

The plight – or social threat – of such homeless and destitute youth in the big cities had long been one of the central themes of the Victorian reforming conscience, and has been recently rediscovered by the mass media in the form of crusading television documentaries such as 'Cathy Come Home'. But such a moralistic stance obscures the changes in both their expectations and their appearance that have occurred among the young migrants themselves. Here is a portrait of one such wanderer of the thirties from an account in the *Daily Herald* in 1934:

This new figure, this modern type of tramp, does not slouch about rural lanes and sleep under haystacks. He is neither old nor dirty. There is nothing furtive about him. He looks ahead of him instead of staring at the ground (with occasional sideways glance), as the 'old-timer' used to do. But there is a strained, almost hounded look on his young features. His once smart suit is shiny, frayed at the sleeves, a little ragged at the trouser-ends. But his hair is always neatly brushed, and somehow or other he manages to keep his shoes clean, no matter how thin the soles may be. He is anything from twenty to twenty-nine years old, and he is walking from town to town, usually with only a few pence in his pocket, looking for work.

This Chaplinesque picture of an itinerant youth in the thirties contrasts sharply with the self-confidence of the beats and hippies of the fifties and sixties, 'on the road' because they consciously wanted to be. He strains after respectability, he develops no life-style or survival network of his own. In the sixties young people congregated around Piccadilly Circus – the Dilly – or Trafalgar Square; in the thirties they met in a modest little set of rooms under Charing Cross railway bridge, the welfare offices of the LCC. Every year over thirty thousand would flock there, nearly 70 per cent of them under the age of twenty-nine.

Thirties youth could scarcely believe that the one-time workshop of the world had no need of its labour. The Unemployed Workers Movement had a militancy tinged with pathos. True to their upbringing the hunger marchers 'tried to be polite all of the time, and say please and thank you when someone offered them a cup of tea'. The Young Socialist 'Right to Work' marchers and the TUC-organized 'Jobs Express' campaigners of recent times scarcely marched straightbacked, in military formation, as their predecessors had done. Instead their ranks included plenty of bright, aggressive punks and rockers. But so far these campaigns have proved an inadequate response to mass unemployment from a Labour movement which, for all the modern militancy of its younger followers, learnt all its tactics in the thirties.

But it is in the attitude to work itself that different generational experiences emerge most clearly. Here a young squatter, a drop-out of the sixties, confronts an old worker who grew up in the thirties.

KID: We are trying to help people. We are trying to create an alternative to the established system.
MAN: When you have done all this, right, you have done all that you want to, and say you win and you do it. Are you going to start work then?
KID: Work? What we are working for is a workless society.
MAN: That means you are not going to work, ever.
KID: We are working for a workless society. Does that make sense to you?
MAN: Not really, no. If you don't work, you don't get food. How are you going to get food then, if you are not working?
KID: Let's take the commune we have organized in Endell Street. That was a building that had been empty for seven years. So obviously it was pretty dirty. Now it's clean. We get things given to us by people who realize what we are about and want to help this thing go forward. We get paint, anything. We can use anything and everything and we get lots of things given by people who know what we are trying to do.

143

MAN: So if everybody is of the same opinion as you and nobody wants to work, then who is going to give who what?

KID: I am not saying we do not want to work. I have no objection to working. I have a very strong objection to working in a meaningless task when I don't need to.

MAN: What *do* you want?

KID: Freedom to be.

MAN: No. To live. What is necessary for you to live?

KID: I need to eat. I need shelter. That's it.

MAN: And you expect the community to provide you with what you need to live, a young bloke like you, twenty-three, twenty-four?

KID: I'm nineteen.

MAN: All right, nineteen. You want the world to keep you because you are too lazy to work ...

The rejection of work and the constraints of a life hedged in on all sides by its disciplines is a luxury confined to those few school-leavers lucky enough to have a choice in the matter. As one teacher points out, 'At school they are told to aim high, to think beyond dull routine work, and then they leave and go on the dole or into insecure government training-schemes (YOPS).' Not to work, and to lose hope in the possibility of a real job for a real wage, is to lose hope in the future altogether. Helen, aged eighteen, has been unemployed since leaving school. She sums up the mood of this generation: 'Now it's all schemes and they don't teach you a thing. You're a YOP. I hate being called a YOP, we all do. Like we're a new bloody species. They come in and say, "These are all YOPs." Like the zoo really. Bit of a laugh, I suppose, but it irritates. You do get bored, but then we're supposed to be bored, ain't we? The newspapers say we're bored teenagers, so if we're supposed to be bored we'll be bored. I've got no *ambitions*, just one ambition, to get a job. I used to cry at night when I was a kid, thinking about it, that there's no future. No young person these days thinks they'll live till they're old ...'

# Across the Soccer Generations

It is hard for one generation to understand the activities and obsessions of another. At football grounds, old men watched in dismay as the kids tore into each other. Many felt resentful at the way *their* game, *their* pastime, was being invaded. Yet only the police, whose job it was, ever felt vested with enough authority to intervene. Thousands of older fans simply stopped going (often never to return, if dramatically falling gates are anything to go by). But some did try to understand, by comparing it with their own youthful experiences.

Ken Livingstone was chairman of Birmingham City Supporters Club, whose main concern is organizing travel to away matches. But there is also a club bar, snooker team, dominoes, table-tennis, and the occasional Sunday night disco, all housed in a few rooms under the St Andrew's ground's main stand.

Now in his seventies, Mr Livingstone can recall 'a more honourable time' for fans, 'when you could go all over the country, London, Manchester, wear your colours, without fear of being physically assaulted'.

'I've been a Birmingham City supporter for fifty years. There was nothing polite about the crowds in the old days.[1] From times I could remember there were scuffles in crowds. But it was punch-ups among *men* in those days. It was different. It was rough all right. But I

1. 'The steps are as greasy as a school playground lavatory in the rain. The air is rancid with beer and belching and worse. The language is a gross purple of obscenity. When the crowd surges at a shot or a collision near a corner flag a man, a boy or sometimes even a girl can be lifted off the ground in the crush as if by some massive, soft-sided crane grab and dangled about for minutes on end, perhaps never getting back to within four or five steps of the spot from which the monster made its bite.' This description of pre-war terrace crowds comes from Arthur Hopcraft's *The Football Man*, Collins, 1968.

don't think the viciousness was in the air then as it is now. It's a more vicious sort of involvement these days. I stood on the Spion Kop. I went every week with the lads my own age, twenty-strong. All down together like, on a Saturday afternoon. I don't think it entered our heads in them days. I can't even recall it passing our minds even. It was always a general mix-up of fans. You did get the odd scuffle, as I said, especially in local derbies. I do remember one or two free-for-alls, but it was not really malicious. It was just a punch-up and that was the end of it.

'We went to watch a game when I was a lad. If I stepped out of line, on or off the terraces, I got a bloody good hiding from my dad and that was it. The game has changed. It's changed in many aspects. Footballers weren't superstars like they are today. In those days they weren't earning much more than the blokes watching them. You get mellow as you get older. You don't get so excited. But basically I think the same excitement's there. You wonder with some of these lads today whether they are really interested in the football as such.

'The young fans now do tend to flock together in their own little areas. First they all went and stood up the Tilton End. Then they disintegrated, split up, and drifted to other parts of the ground. It's mainly on the Kop, the popular side, that they congregate now. On one occasion, some of these young fans, only thirteen or fourteen years old they were, were involved in a scuffle with an old man selling programmes. They just snatched the programmes off him. I recognized this one lad. I know his father very well. I told his father, "You wanna have a word with him," and he could have thumped me! He just couldn't believe it had happened. He said, "You are gonna stand there and tell me my son did that?" That boy was a well-behaved sort of person in his own home. But it's when he gets involved with people in his own age group, and in numbers, it seems to – it's like a different person altogether.

'There are a lot of good kids like that among the ones who get in trouble. But the hard core, the really destructive element, are they really football fans? You've got to break that lot up. You could close every ground in the country, they would still be making trouble somewhere.

'We had a very big exercise carried out by the police at the Tilton

End: TV-monitoring, plainclothes policemen mingling with the crowd. That way we did manage to eliminate a few of the ringleaders. They're like sheep, some of them. They will follow any leader. I think the players can give a lead here instead. The most impressionable thing on youngsters is the appearance of the players. If every player devoted a couple of hours a week to encourage the lads, a word from them would have more effect than anybody. I would also like to see a lot more time and space through the media on highlighting the best parts of being a football supporter. I would certainly like to see the Federation of Supporters Clubs more widely recognized. We have a hell of a fight to get represented on any working party of any description. The people who run football would as soon shut their eyes as though we weren't there. A lot of ideas could be channelled through supporters clubs, ideas for improving the game based on what the people themselves are thinking. Football clubs seem to frown on any official bodies being set up which they haven't got direct control over. We've got to remind them; their business is the general public. At present there is not that much that we can really offer the kids. Most stadiums were built so many years ago that they can't really incorporate improvements. At St Andrew's we have a room if the kids want to play table-tennis. But it isn't big enough. The state of grounds like this is pretty desperate. Football clubs could give a more positive lead, though, encouraging people, rather than turning away, head in the air, saying, "Hooliganism might go away if we turn our backs on it."'

'In Manchester, life is divided between work and football. And the prospects for both look pretty bleak.' Ric Sumner, aged fifty, a former welder, runs a community centre in Moss Side. A lifelong Manchester City supporter, he continues to follow the game and helps to organize young people in his neighbourhood. He is therefore better qualified than most to comment on the long battle as it has taken place on his terrace and in his community, and which I have tried to describe.

*'When did you first go to Maine Road?'*

'About 1939, and I went sporadically through the war. I used to go to watch from the scoreboard end for years and years, before they built the new North Stand. I stood there for donkey's years behind the goal. Now the crowd go to Platt's Lane to stand, which is down the side. I went with my big brother. He's one of the rare cases who defected. He went over to the Reds![1] He went in the navy and came out corrupted. [*Laughs*.] But all the rest of my family have always been City supporters.

'Up until the North Stand was built, when I used to stand behind the goal, it was a very mixed crowd. There was a lot of old blokes, and women, even some elderly women. You all stood there together. You knew everybody. You never saw 'em between games. But we always stood in roughly the same place and we knew the forty or fifty people around us cos they were always there. The worst hazard of standing in that crowd was someone pissing down the back of your leg. But now it's getting a bottle on your head and that's a different thing altogether. It takes the fun out of it. [*Laughs*.]

'I don't think it ever occurred to us to fight on the terraces. I remember when I was seventeen, and my brother, who was a big lad, bigger than me – and the old fella's a bit smaller than both of us, and he was stood in front of us. And got into an argument with a bloke. It almost came to blows. So we stepped forward and said, "'Ere, leave 'im alone like." Now that really stuck in my head. It was nothing! It never came to blows or anything, but it came very close to blows, and that was the first time I'd ever really seen anybody come close to violence at a match. It was years and years after before I saw any real aggro. Yet the crowds then were as big as now, if not bigger. Violence was almost unknown. Of course we used to fight in pubs. [*Laughs*.] I mean, I remember the occasional punch-up with other supporters in a pub, but it wasn't really related to the football. It was more like "This is our pub. What are you fellas doing in here? Go back to Sunderland or wherever." But it wasn't regular by any means. It was just now and again.

'Above all, you went to see a good game of football. I've seen times when the team's won, and I've been sick at the terrible football they've played. I've seen 'em lose and it's been such a superb game of football that you didn't care. All right, it's better your team win, but to see a good game of football is more important to me than

1. Manchester United.

to see my team win. And that's dying too. I don't think many people
go with that attitude any more – particularly the kids. There's a
lot of explanations, there's lot of frustrations ... Kids now have
got a worse time than we had. The families might be better off, but
they have a worse life, I think ... Where they were born, old neighbourhoods of Manchester have been smashed up and their communities scattered to the four winds. People move on to a new estate.
There isn't an established society there. There isn't anything for 'em
to fit into. The kids come along – you got a couple of hundred
teenagers roaming a newly built area. And all they can do to prove
themselves is to be better vandals than anybody else.

'I mean some of them are amazing vandals. I work in East
Manchester, and the imagination of these kids – it's incredible. At
one stage they were actually *gaining* on the building workers who
were putting up the estate. By the end of the week there was less
built than there had been on the Monday. They wrecked lifts, they
burnt out their motors. They didn't just smash them up. They would
rig up scaffolding and then switch the lift on, so that the cables
would break and the motor would burn out. And these were bright,
intelligent kids.

'Why do they do it? Look at the concrete flats outside 'ere! Can
you imagine anybody looking at them and getting a warm glow and
saying, "That's home!" We used to have that in the old – what they
told us were slums. I mean at least you felt you were home when
you walked down the street. You were somebody. You got a place,
you got an identity. Everybody knew you.

'When I was a kid there was this old cripple who was a rag and
bone man. But we didn't make fun of him cos we'd grow up and
he'd always be there. You knew who he was. I wonder what happens
to blokes like that after the bulldozers come and he's dumped in
an area with kids who didn't grow up with 'im ... A figure of fun ...

'I grew up in Moss Side and it was a tough place when I grew
up, but there were certain codes. In the area if anybody did a gas
meter, you know, they might as well go and live somewhere else,
they were finished. If they took an old lady's purse they were gonna
get their legs broken. Cos the community – the villains and the real
thieves in the community – had a certain code. Maybe not a code
that was acceptable to society at large, but it functioned in this area.

149

And if you wanted to go and rob someone's house, you went to Cheadle, or Gatley, or Didsbury, where there was something worth taking, and no way did you rob a working-class guy because he didn't have anything and he was like you and that was very much a community-imposed code. But of course that community was destroyed, and those kinds of codes were destroyed, and we've got a situation now where kids don't have any code at all, don't have any loyalty at all, except to a very, very small group of mates of maybe a dozen. And even within that group, you know, they'll go and grass on each other. Now when I was a kid, if anybody had gone and grassed to the police they'd've got the next bus out of town, cos that was it. It was a hard and violent community, but it had its code, it had certain things you didn't do, and you didn't rob old ladies, and you didn't do gas meters, and you didn't grass on your mates.

'Now I've got season-tickets, for seats behind the goal. I suppose that makes me some kind of millionaire. But you get a good view of the game, and that community feeling, you can still get a bit of that now, in the seats. You've got to sit with the same people every week. You do get to know them and you do get to know the kids. There's whole families go into our Park Lane stand. But twenty years ago, the thought of sitting down to watch a football match would have seemed ludicrous to me. I even had a mate who had two season-tickets – he was a nightclub owner – and he always used to stand with us on the terrace, and he used to give his tickets away to business acquaintances as a goodwill thing. He used to say, "Ah, you can't sit down to watch a match." He's in his seat now as well.'

# Training Diary

In September 1983, the government launched a new, billion-pound Youth Training Scheme designed to provide 'quality training' for a half a million school-leavers who have nowhere else to go but on the dole. YTS replaces the much-criticized YOPs (Youth Opportunities Programmes). When it was introduced I was working as an instructor in a training workshop in North-West London, one place that offers more than just training as an excuse for keeping kids off the streets.

I offer this extract from my diary as an example of what can happen in a workshop which is geared to the needs of young people.

*5 September*: After the long wait since leaving school, you would think that Delroy Williams would be relieved to get a place at New Start Skill Centre. Instead, he looks sullen and anxious. I try to sound encouraging.

'In your application, Delroy, you said you wanted to train as a plumber. We will give you every chance. Jerry Forbes will be your supervisor. The hours are nine to five. The pay is twenty-five pounds a week.' Through my office window I can see a trainee, a slightly built lad, gamely trying to steer a heavy wheelbarrow up a ramp.

'There are hopes of a pay rise,' I went on. 'Most trainees at New Start are in a union. They have been trying to put pressure on the local Council for a ten-pound-a-week top-up. Read the rules carefully before signing. If there is anything you want to know, just ask.'

'Look,' said Delroy, 'I wanna start, bad. But ... I'm in a lot of shit. I'm on a charge. Assault with intent to rob. Serious.'

It turned out that Delroy, in company with some older youths, had, while playing truant from school, attempted to rob a sub-post-office. He was supposed to cut the telephone wires. Instead, he had got locked in the shop when the alarm was raised. I told Delroy

151

he would get time off to sort out this matter. Provided he tried hard and kept out of trouble, his solicitors could approach us for a reference.

*8 September:* Lorraine Coles has just joined YTS, and wants to concentrate on typing and secretarial work. How about a traditional man's trade, such as carpentry, I suggest.

'I like to look after my appearance. I don't want to end up every day covered in sawdust, looking like a scarecrow.'

She acknowledges that girls could do as well as men in carpentry: 'Better, most probably. Girls are superior to men; they are less silly. Boys just want to muck about most of the time.'

I ask Lorraine how she had heard of New Start. 'Through my mates. They said it was all right. My older sister goes out with a boy who came here. He said it was a good place.'

*12 September:* The official Careers Office brochure says that New Start is run like a model factory. But one visitor described it as 'more like a happy farm'. An independent research report describes New Start as 'informal but purposeful, and relations between staff and trainees are good-humoured and based on mutual respect'.

*15 September:* Eddie Butterworth came in this morning sporting a Mohican hair-cut. The other trainees call him Bootlaces – from Eddie Shoestring, TV detective. Eddie wants to be a bricklayer, like his dad. When I explain that I am responsible for his 'off-the-job' training – and that includes reading, writing and maths – Eddie gets impatient. 'I had enough of that at school. I come here to lay bricks, to get used to a trowel. At school they just learn yer things. I wanna *do* things.' I say to him that you don't get to be a bricklayer overnight. While you are training, it does no harm to improve reading, writing and estimating figures. Eddie agrees to think about it.

*19 September:* In an Open Forum Delroy reports that the worst thing about New Start is having to get up in the morning to get in on time. The best thing is going out on jobs, such as fixing taps and draining a central-heating system. Lorraine is getting fed up with taking sexist jibes from some of the boys, although she can give as good as she gets. The other day she called Eddie 'a facety little white boy'.

*20 September:* Eddie gets into an argument with another trainee, who, he claims, is 'taking liberties'. Blows are exchanged. The dispute is quickly broken up by supervisors with the help of trainees. Eddie is hauled up before the manager who tells him that violence in any form will not be tolerated. Anyone who raises a hand, a tool, in anger is normally dismissed on the spot. Eddie pleads extreme provocation, and points out that no one got hurt. 'All I want is respect,' he claims. He is told: 'If you give respect, you will get it. If you don't, you may as well leave.' Eddie is given leave to appeal against dismissal.

*21 September:* Delroy's case finally comes up. He is sentenced to a short, sharp shock – a minimum of six weeks at a detention centre, subject to good behaviour. He requests that we keep his place in the plumbing section open, so that he can return to us in December.

*27 September:* Two men, with beards and leather jackets, stand outside the gates of New Start and try to flog copies of *Workers Forward!* to the trainees. They tell the kids that they are 'being exploited as a reserve army of cheap labour for capitalism'.

*21 October:* A meeting with Tony Dhokes, manager of the nearby Breakwell Industrial Training Workshop. He is an ex-army officer, who wears a white coat and carries a clip-board. He has been attempting quasi time-and-motion studies of trainees, but is disappointed with the results.

'Teach them a skill? Make them useful members of society? That's all very well in theory . . . Let's face it, most of the Mode B [Voluntary Training Workshop] youngsters we get cannot even cross the road without getting lost. What good are they to prospective employers? The mad, the bad and the sad, that's my trainees. The best you can say for YTS is that it is keeping them off the streets, so that they are not such a danger to the public.'

I point out that there are thousands of young people leaving school with little hope and not much self-esteem. It is our task to make a serious attempt to provide them with real skills, not endless assessment forms. Working-class youth is being forced into a position of wildness and irresponsibility. This process has been going on since the sixties . . .

Dhokes asks if there have been any cases of sabotage at New Start. He mentions supervisors' cars wrecked at Breakwell, fire-extinguishers deliberately let off, tools and technical equipment vandalized. Could Youth Training Schemes become new centres of youth revolt?

*23 December:* Christmas dinner at New Start. Afterwards I talk with Delroy, who has returned; Eddie, whose appeal to be kept on was upheld; and Lorraine, who is leaving to get a job in an advertising office. Delroy reports that the short, sharp shock was 'a holiday', full of cross-country runs at five-thirty in the morning in the freezing cold, and plenty of kicks and punches from frustrated screws. A holiday was it?

I ask Eddie if he is going down White Hart Lane over the holidays – he is a Spurs fan. 'I dunno. There's too many coppers. You don't have no rows there now. The coppers jump yer as soon as you start. These days you have to go out of London to have rows. You have to go abroad for it. Like the Spurs did in Rotterdam. And the England fans in Denmark, Switzerland – places like that.'

Lorraine tells us about her job. The company has offered to put her on a course to learn word-processing with computers. She estimates that she will soon be earning over a hundred pounds a week. Meanwhile she is going to vote Conservative in the future: 'Mrs Thatcher is good for this country. We all know Labour is useless.' She heard on television that the economy was on the upturn and that there would soon be loads more jobs for youth. This is greeted by the others with snorts of derision. I remind them all that, according to the public-opinion polls, the swing to the right in the June election was every bit as marked among young people as elsewhere. Delroy cannot believe it. I mention the Tory Festival of Youth at election time, where Kenny Everett's call to 'Bomb Russia' drew hysterical applause and Thatcher told her Young Conservatives that 'The future is ours.' 'Sounds like the Nuremberg Rallies,' says Eddie.

Local community-based initiatives like New Start are the exception rather than the rule, however. The broader picture is darker.

# End Piece

The underlying social inequalities have sharpened since the early sixties. Young people have been more severely affected by the recession than any other group. According to figures supplied by the independent campaigning organization, Youthaid, the rate of unemployment among the under-twenty-fives is twice that of older people. Apart from those on Youth Training Schemes (some 300,000 at present), there are 1.2 million under-twenty-fives out of work, over 540,000 of them in their teens. About a quarter of them have been out of work for more than a year.

If it achieves little else, YTS does reduce the size of the labour force, by raising to seventeen the age of entry into the labour market. For the youth research industry, training replaces youth culture as the main cause for concern.

Cynics would suggest that YTS is largely an attempt by government to 'magic away' part of those damaging unemployment figures. During the 1983 election campaign, government think-tank documents were leaked to *Time Out* magazine: 'We estimate the training year (YTS) would reduce the level of registered unemployment by about 200,000 above the 130,000 (reduction) resulting from YOP (Youth Opportunities Programme).'

YTS also represents a major attempt by the state to modify 'anti-social' and irresponsible forms of youthful behaviour. YTS 'social skills' and 'off-the-job' training aim to replace the world of We Hate Humans with more socially acceptable attitudes, such as responsibility and concern for others and a willingness to conform. And, in return, working-class youth are given vague promises of new technology leading to upturns in the economy, followed by greater job opportunities 'in the future'. But when? Independent economic forecasts continue to be gloomy.

So far organized youth resistance to unemployment has been minimal. But what happens if a whole generation discovers it has been in training for nothing?

## MORE ABOUT PENGUINS, PELICANS
## AND PUFFINS

For further information about books available from Penguins please write to Dept EP, Penguin Books Ltd, Harmondsworth, Middlesex UB7 0DA.

*In the U.S.A.*: For a complete list of books available from Penguins in the United States write to Dept DG, Penguin Books, 299 Murray Hill Parkway, East Rutherford, New Jersey 07073.

*In Canada*: For a complete list of books available from Penguins in Canada write to Penguin Books Canada Ltd, 2801 John Street, Markham, Ontario L3R 1B4.

*In Australia*: For a complete list of books available from Penguins in Australia write to the Marketing Department, Penguin Books Australia Ltd, P.O. Box 257, Ringwood, Victoria 3134.

*In New Zealand*: For a complete list of books available from Penguins in New Zealand write to the Marketing Department, Penguin Books (N.Z.) Ltd, P.O. Box 4019, Auckland 10.

*In India*: For a complete list of books available from Penguins in India write to Penguin Overseas Ltd, 706 Eros Apartments, 56 Nehru Place, New Delhi 110019.

## KNUCKLE SANDWICH
*Growing up in the working-class city*
*David Robins and Philip Cohen*

*Knuckle Sandwich* is the story of the rise and fall of the Black Horse disco. In a dilapidated pub in the centre of a working-class estate, kids and youth workers attempted to find an alternative to ping-pong and ineffectual youth clubs, to boredom and violence. The disco was a success until the kids began to demand live bands, tenants complained and gangs from other estates turned up. Boredom and violence came back

'At a time of rising juvenile unemployment, the authors well catch the general mood of nihilistic, violent despair among the young and they emphasize over and over again the political economy of their predicament' – *The Times Educational Supplement*

## PASSAGE TO BRITAIN
*James Walvin*

Informed and cogently argued, *Passage to Britain* combines historical documentary with a new agenda for the eighties. James Walvin applies a fresh eye to three key issues. He provides the context by tracing the history of immigration to Britain since the Middle Ages; he discusses recent events – legislation since 1962, political initiatives, organizations from the Campaign for Racial Equality to the National Front; and he gives us a flavour of the grim and frustrating realities for those living in Britain's 'mosaic of communities'.

Largely because of Britain's loss of Empire and diminishing world influence, the age-old controversy over immigration has hardened into a major political issue. Here the acrimonious debate about race and colour is discussed and illustrated to show how it touches on all the areas of current social concern. Teachers, legislators, politicians, activists and everyone working towards racial equality in Britain will find that *Passage to Britain* gives a constructive new impetus to the question: What can be done?

## WHAT IS TO BE DONE ABOUT...?

These short and simple books, published in connection with the Socialist Society, will deal with the central social and political issues of the day. They will set out the arguments, provide information and answer important questions, offering a political agenda for the eighties.

## WHAT IS TO BE DONE ABOUT THE FAMILY?
*Lynne Segal*

The protective nuclear family seems to be breaking down: the divorce rate is high, children are alienated from parents, the old are neglected. Here the authors explain and argue exactly *why* it is crucial for the future of society that the issues surrounding the family become subject to political analysis and action.

## WHAT IS TO BE DONE ABOUT LAW AND ORDER?
*John Lea and*
*Jock Young*

What is *meant* by law and order? Whose law and what order? This timely study examines all the issues, discussing the concept of a 'breakdown of society', the present threat to our liberty, and what is to be done about the increasingly confrontational nature of forces within society in the British Isles.

*Other books in this series will discuss the environment, health care, higher education, NATO, and violence against women.*